PITKIN COUNTY
library
inspire growth

PITKIN COUNTY LIBRARY

S0-CBT-247

120 North Mill Street • Aspen, CO 81611 • 970-429-1900

FICTION B6574ni   28.00
Bloxam, M. F., 1958-
The night batt...

WITHDRAWN

The
Night Battles

The
Night Battles

M.F. BLOXAM

THE PERMANENT PRESS
Sag Harbor, NY 11963

The text of Giuseppe Gisira's interrogation is quoted from Carlo Ginzburg, *The Night Battles: Witches and Agrarian Cults in the Sixteenth and Seventeenth Centuries*, Baltimore, with permission from The Johns Hopkins University Press (1983), pp. 153–4.

Giulio Cesare Croce's poem is quoted from Piero Camporesi, *Bread of Dreams*, Chicago, with permission from The University of Chicago Press (1989), p. 128.

Copyright © 2008 M.F. Bloxam.

All rights reserved. No part of this publication, or parts thereof, may be reproduced in any form, except for the inclusion of brief quotes in a review, without the written permission of the publisher.

For information, address:
The Permanent Press
4170 Noyac Road
Sag Harbor, NY 11963
www.thepermanentpress.com

Library of Congress Cataloging-in-Publication Data

Bloxam, M. F.-
    The night battles / M.F. Bloxam.
        p. cm.
    ISBN-13: 978-1-57962-171-1 (alk. paper)
    ISBN-10: 1-57962-171-6 (alk. paper)
        1. Women historians—Fiction. 2. Sicily (Italy)—Fiction.
    3. Psychological fiction. I. Title.

    PS3602.L68N54 2008
    813'.6—dc22   2008024815

Printed in the United States of America.

For

KFH

ACKNOWLEDGEMENTS

One writes in solitude; one succeeds in the company of friends. I have many, many to thank: the New Hampshire State Council on the Arts; Jodie Rhodes; Martin and Judith Shepard and the wonderful production staff at The Permanent Press; Christina Ward; Dot Radius Kasik; Beth Hartnett; John Robinson; the Downtown Book Club; and family, friends and neighbors. James Vopat has my special gratitude. I have been most fortunate.

Having so vast a cloud of witnesses surrounding us, let us lay aside every weight, and run with perseverance the race set before us.

(Hebrews 12:1)

I have sometimes gone out of doors,
And have lost myself in caverns and caves,
And have talked several times with Death.

One moment I ride on the back of a ram,
Another I seem to mount a dolphin;
Now on an elephant, or a lion.

Almost every day I dream I am flying . . .

— GULIO CESARE CROCE
Sogni fantastichi della notte, 1629

CHAPTER ONE

The archives are what bring me to Valparuta.

I first meet Cosimo Chiesa there, among the books and manuscripts of Valparuta's library.

It's late June when I arrive, and I've forgotten what it's like in Sicily at solstice, the thick air and white light, the pressing sun. I'm not ready for it. At Aidone in midsummer the harvested wheatfields were like drained lakes and the oleander blossoms had blown, but what comes back to me now is my mother's darkened flat in Palermo on the Feast of St. John the Baptist, the neighbor girls peering into a basin of water set on the floor, a lit candle nearby. They are looking in the water for their future husbands' faces. One girl sees instead a vast legion of men, she thinks they're Muslims; some ride horses and others have no hands. She shrieks and scoots away. Breathless, giggling, the others dare to look. They cup their palms over their mouths, ready for wonders.

This is what I remember of the Sicilian solstice.

The ornate gloom of Palermo's *Biblioteca Comunale* comes back to me, too, since I've returned to Sicily for the archives.

The *Biblioteca* stood behind the Jesuit church, an angry Baroque wedding-cake the priests had frosted on the inside rather than out. My mother and I could walk there from her condemned building in the Kalsa, and often did, my mother searching the old newspapers there for hours, hunting up Palermo's secrets. She'd occupied that decayed apartment of hers to save it from the wrecking crews, a mad enterprise; she'd set herself and her photograph files down in the bulldozers' path and dared the city to molest her. The librarians at the *Biblioteca* knew she was *L'Ora*'s crime scene photographer and an activist, a troublemaker of the worst sort, and would not assist her. I remember their shrugs and their blank faces, my mother's raised voice. I would live in libraries now if I could, but my mother's crumbling squat, Palermo's decrepit mausoleum and its evil staff are not the reasons why.

I want to know if all that has been claimed of Valparuta's archives is true.

But instead I'm hijacked. It's June 23; I've been back in Sicily for less than sixteen hours. I left it twenty-five years ago, when my father finally took me away for good. Everything here is at once familiar to me and utterly strange. The heat is mythic, pervasive.

It's the feast day of St. John the Baptist.

Mayor Giuseppe Agretta himself takes charge of my abduction, a grand welcoming tour of Valparuta's *città vecchia*. He is a vastly enthusiastic guide, speeding up the steep cobbled streets in his gorgeous suit, trailing secretaries and minor officials like a comet. He shows me every ogee-arched doorway in the old Arab quarter, all the eroded Trees of Jesse in the old Jewish quarter; he runs us all gasping up to the Norman *rocca*. His Italian is torrential, its consonants melted down to fit a Sicilian mouth. I should be many foreign dignitaries, it seems, not one lone researcher; the mayor lectures me as if I were a delegation. He doesn't know that I've seen all this before somewhere else, a long time ago. He doesn't know that throughout his cascading talk I'm looking into a basin of water, seeing other bricked-up loggias and crumbling *palazzi*. I let two hours pass this way. I'm due at the library at one o'clock to meet Signor Chiesa but I don't care, I'll slight Valparuta's archivist to repay those Palermitan librarians. I'm consulting my memories and they are oracular, open to interpretation. They may or may not have anything to say about the months I mean to spend here in Valparuta.

Mayor Agretta opens his arms to embrace the peeling Baroque facades around us. "Who else on this island can present so medieval an aspect, eh?" he cries. "Who else has retained their history wholesale, as we have? I tell you, *Professoressa*—we are honored that you are the first, the first of many who will surely come here for our treasures!"

He outdistances us again, his midnight-colored suit black as soot against the sun. In my mind I have Palermo's dressed pavements underfoot, not Valparuta's irregular cobbles, and so I stumble once. A young woman with a mass of hair like ravelled rope leans close.

"Are you all right, *Professoressa*?" she whispers. She is fabulously *alla moda*, wrapped in a raw silk blouse and waist-less delaine miniskirt that somehow fails to hinder her; she navigates the cobbled street effortlessly in high heels. But her painted mouth is set like one who has lost an argument—this long hot morning on the streets does not please her. She wishes me to put an end to it.

11

I tell her that I'm fine, *grazie*, the sun was in my eyes. I'm wearing Ray-Bans. She leaves me in disgust.

Mayor Agretta is welcome to his happy prophesies. We all see what we wish for on St. John's Day if we're lucky, and damn those who don't keep their skepticism to themselves.

For the truth is that Valparuta is a bleak place, a small fortress city crammed atop a lone calcareous bluff—plagued by chill and fogs in winter, no doubt, and blasted dry in summer. No amount of optimism can save it from itself. Every defensible height in Sicily is built up in this way, Norman fort heaped upon Roman, Roman on Greek. Narrow houses are built one on the next of scavenged temple fragments and funerary tablets, the entire accretion cinched in by thick walls and the edges of cliffs. Russell—my careless father—still has an enviable contempt for hill towns like this one, and I'll allow it; *you can't tell what the hell was going on in places like that,* he told me once. Bluffs like Valparuta's make magpies of people— they carry everything off to use again and again, it's nothing but building material to them. Russell hated all the stacked-up living floors and superimposed horizons, found four millennia of continuous occupation a nuisance. But I'm here for excavations of another sort, the unearthing of written records. Valparuta is just an unremarkable hinterland as far as I'm concerned, a welter of diminished, vernacular architecture halfway between earth and sky. At the height we've reached the city seems built entirely of cobbles kicked up by ancient plows and hauled laboriously up the cliff. There's a sense of impermanence here, as if the ill-made walls and stepped streets have lasted longer than anyone meant them to.

More odd dull piazzas, dim churches and truncated campaniles. We reach the windy, uppermost region of the city; Mayor Agretta pauses at last, casts about for something more to show me.

A young aide, a skinny determined boy in stylish clothes, speaks up from the edge of the group. "Signor Agretta— Your Honor—there isn't any more," he says, and gives me a killing look.

Mayor Agretta frowns at his watch like a man who's slept too long, but his dismay is false.

"Eh, Holy Jesus and all the saints!" he cries, smacking a palm to his forehead. "It's nearly one-thirty—Emedio, why didn't you say something?"

Emedio, the skinny boy with the angry stare, only shrugs.

"I was to have the *Professoressa* at the library by one o'clock!" the mayor cries. "Signor Chiesa is missing his lunch—he'll be furious with me!"

And so he leads us all back downhill in a terrible hurry, sometimes forgetting himself and hopping like a boy down the steps of the steepest streets.

We straggle into the deserted main piazza. It's not much— a small, uneven plain of patterned cobbles with no central monument or *parco*, not even an ornamented public cistern installed to weather sieges. Tall *palazzi* stand like fortifications on all sides, housing city offices, shops and *caffè* bars. The sun strikes their high yellow facades with such force that I expect the sound of hammers. From open casements and shadowed doorways comes the rapid murmur of men's voices, plates chiming. The heavy scent of pounded basil and garlic throws me back again, to a cold summer lunch of *pasta alla carrettiera*, eaten in silence at my mother's parents' farm in Aidone; and to my mother spooning *ammogghiu* over egg-plant grilled on her bedroom balcony—the one that finally fell into the street.

Mayor Agretta's retinue has somehow vanished. The library towers precipitously before me now, its complex face radiating heat. I have an impression of heavy scrollwork, colonettes and rusticated friezes, all effaced by intolerable light. I close my eyes against it, feel myself fall briefly toward darkness—and yank myself back up.

The mayor leans into me as I pass him through the door. "Never mind Signor Chiesa," he says. "He will simply have to excuse us, eh?"

I smile sweetly, take off my sunglasses and let him see my eyes. "I'm going to blame you, Signor Agretta," I say, and watch his face rearrange itself.

I'm ready for the Palermo library's stunted twin—ill-lit stacks and rotting books shelved every which way, walls of bloody-looking porphyry—but Valparuta's *Biblioteca Comunale* surprises me. I'm standing in the atrium of a bright, reasonably airy hall occupied by reading tables. Orderly metal stacks are set in galleries all around, and more stacks are visible through the upper gallery's heavy marble balustrade. A grand, curved staircase rises at the back of the hall. The floors are of pale grey marble, the walls the same, the stacks are grey; Valparuta's library is like a mind just wakened in the morning, calm, largely clear, ready for the day's first impressions. I like it immediately.

The tables are all empty.

"Oh," says Mayor Agretta, "no doubt Signor Chiesa sent everyone out long ago. We're late, late!"

He slips past me at a businessman's run, that rapid, self-important walk that executives all over the world have mastered, heading for the marble staircase. "Signor Chiesa, Signor Chiesa—we're here!" he sings out, as if we've all been at a game of hide-and-seek. His voice dies strangely when it strikes the ranks of books.

Mayor Agretta is halfway up the stairs when Chiesa appears above him. The archivist has just put on his suitcoat, a handsome thing—he's still rolling his shoulders to make

14

it set properly. The coat hangs badly on him, even from where I stand. He's taken a heavier colleague's coat by mistake, I think.

The mayor stops on the stairs, suddenly tentative. "Ah, Signor Chiesa," he says. "There you are."

"Yes," says Chicsa. "But where have you been?"

The mayor doesn't answer. Instead he seizes Chiesa's elbow and propels him down the stairs to me, talking all the while about supply requisitions and budget difficulties, a work order held up in contract negotiations. He breaks off suddenly.

"Here is *Professoressa* Severance, Joan Severance!" the mayor cries with a flourish, struggling valiantly with all the strange consonants.

Chiesa is still buttoning his suitcoat, still wrestling the problem of the budget difficulties. He doesn't know what the mayor is talking about; he looks confused and irritated. Hurriedly, he takes my hand in his. His hand is cool and dry, full of bones; his grip is too hard.

Like his library, Chiesa is not what I'm expecting. These plummy civil service jobs go to the well-connected, the troublesome uncles and moneyed friends of those they've put in office. There's nothing of the veteran intriguer about Chiesa, nothing provincial. He's a youngish man, scarcely older than myself, and he has the look of an ascetic, handsomely turned out but too thin and too still. He smells of unfiltered cigarettes and expensive toiletries. The coat he wears is his, I see, not someone else's. He's lost some twenty pounds, I think, and recently; his lapel-less suit is still the height of fashion. He was a slim man even before his weight loss.

And he's no friend of Agretta's. There's a jangling tension between them that's too visceral for dislike. If they had hackles they'd be standing on end—but instead there's this hypocrisy from Agretta and Chiesa's studious calm. I wish now that I hadn't kept Chiesa waiting, thinking him as contemptible as those others.

"*Piacere*," Chiesa says, crushing my fingers.

"Signor Chiesa," I reply. We clinch like trapeze artists, catch each other in midair.

We see the mayor off. He wants to get away from us but can't bring himself to leave; he throws out an anchor of conversation and then drags it behind him toward the door, talking, talking. He assures me again of my unconditional welcome, warns Chiesa not to disappoint me. There will be hell to pay, he says, if it gets back to him that the *Professoressa* isn't happy! He shows his teeth in a lightless smile; he isn't kidding. Chiesa walks him down to the library's enclosed vestibule and gets him through the door, but there in that overheated space the mayor is moved to make a speech. It's a new day in Valparuta, he tells us feelingly, his hand over his heart. His dream of *riprìstino*, of civic revival for Valparuta, has become reality. My presence here assures it—soon there will be tourists and scholars, galleries and *ristoranti*, symposia and festivals throughout the city. Behind him the empty piazza's blazing desert contradicts every word he says.

Chiesa waits it out patiently, his head bowed and his hands clasped behind his back. In the pouring sunlight his suit is reddish-black, the color of oxblood. We could be standing in a terrarium, the vestibule is so close and still.

Agretta wrings my hand, takes Chiesa's without enthusiasm. We watch the mayor speed away across the piazza.

Chiesa sighs, a deep exhalation that ends in a ropy cough. "He kept you deliberately," he says.

"I permitted it," I tell him.

He looks at me closely. "Our town is of great interest to you, then," he says. "We're very fortunate."

I press a palm to my forehead. It feels like a heated cobble. "No, you're not," I say. "I was busy consulting San Giovanni Battista."

Chiesa starts visibly, stills himself again. He must be wondering, all at once, if I might be one of them—an Italian, at least—and not the cachet-laden American *professoressa* they've been expecting. But he is a gentleman; he keeps it to himself. "Well," he says. "The saint was of assistance to you, I hope."

"I was speaking figuratively, Signor Chiesa," I say.

"But you know the tradition."

"I've run across it in my studies," I say. I don't want to tell him of my years in Sicily. They've come on me here like a fever, and may yet pass; I'm not sure that I will have to live with them.

Chiesa seems aware of neither the vestibule's heat nor his lack of hospitality, and we continue to stand together on the big woolen doormat. He's probably like this with books, too—standing for hours in dim, airless stacks with his desk just a few steps away, arrested by words on a page. He is reading me now like a text. I work to turn his gaze aside.

"Mayor Agretta has great plans for Valparuta," I say, and watch his thoughts shift.

Chiesa shrugs. "They got him elected," he says. "No one wanted to be left behind."

"Do you think he'll succeed?"

He gives me a prickly, impatient look. "Do you?" he says.

I don't. Yet Chiesa has tied himself and his archives to this legless plan of the mayor's.

He knows what I'm thinking. "This collection stands on its own merits, *Professoressa*—researchers will come here whether or not we build another hotel or cook up some silly festival for tourists. But there was funding available through the mayor's new *commissione*—a great deal of funding. I wanted it for my archives."

"You petitioned the *commissione*."

He grins suddenly. "I left them convinced that it was I who'd done them the real favor—all those spendthrift foreign eggheads waiting to be lured here for research, staying on for weeks, crowding the *pensioni*, eating and drinking like camels. Agretta isn't the only one who can talk a dog out of his bone."

I take him in as if he were a particularly fine sky. "They'll never see it, what you've promised."

"No. But the archives have been funded."

I reach out then, take Chiesa's sleeve between my fingers. "Show me your archives, will you?" I say.

I've passed some kind of test. "I'd be delighted," Chiesa says.

And this is when I see it. He looks at me straight on, with the sun full in his face, and his pupils are blown wide open.

The archivist is cranking something. There's no other sign that he's high.

It gives Chiesa's face a strange drowned beauty, like a woman with belladonna in her eyes.

Chapter Two

It's Paul Vergone who tells me about Valparuta's archives.

I first entered his proximity when he and I team-taught a 100-level course on the European Union—a throwaway class peopled by thirty-two distracted students: marginal Marketing majors, overloaded pre-meds with the smell of chem lab on their clothes, the usual rabble of perplexed Undeclareds, and a few determinedly hostile Anthropology majors—students of mine wearing mall-bought Guatemalan cotton, come to monitor my behavior in this dubious capitalist course.

They were right to suspect me. Paul Vergone and I had eyed each other for months as we passed in our shared hallway, circling one another warily like a dog and cat, mindful of the other's territory. He was dangerously attractive, a tense, self-assured man who dressed in dark turtlenecks and wide-wale corduroys, wore his black hair over his collar and affected steel-rimmed glasses. His abrupt smile revealed crowded teeth.

Thrown together in that class, we practiced subtle defamation before our unwitting audience, calling principles of the other's discipline into question, maligning intent, philosophy, world view, scholarship—everything. He was better at it than I. I heard that he was recently divorced, that he'd come to Brown to put several states between himself and his ex-wife. But he had not yet lost the habits of an emotional pugilist, the guarding and the sudden blows. I would have liked to have studied his ex-wife from across a crowded room; she must have been a formidable opponent.

Enmity makes friends of its own. That class left Vergone and me to acknowledge each other daily with nods and chilly smiles in the hallway between our offices, holding the other's eyes too long as we passed. We were like unrepentant sinners, faced with our crimes. We would do it all again in an instant, given the opportunity.

"Joan," Vergone says one day, and it's an afterthought, something he remembers after we've shown each other our teeth in the hallway one winter afternoon. A heavy snow is brewing, it's a Friday; students have fled early for the weekend. Somehow I feel even more reckless, more willing to tangle with Vergone, knowing that there is no good reason for either of us to be here, prowling empty halls.

Particularly in my case. I haven't taught a class in weeks; I've been relieved of my teaching duties. I come here just because I can—no one has found the courage yet to tell me to stay away.

I turn back to Vergone, keep the distance he's left between us.

"Some archives in Sicily were just opened to researchers," he says. "I saw an article in *Il Corrière*. They sounded pretty interesting—your kind of thing."

"I don't care about Sicily."

He frowns with false perplexity. "Wasn't your mother from there?"

"And my father is from California. I don't study it."

"I thought you grew up there, too. In Sicily." He doesn't look away when he says this.

"I lived there until I was seven," I tell him. Those three summers that followed—the ones spent with my mother in Palermo—are laid in rock with all the others; I won't undertake their excavation for him. "I grew up here," I say. But he nods as if he has taken some information from this that I did not mean to give him. "I'll put it in your mailbox," he says.

"Don't bother."

"No, I will," he says, grinning now. "It really is your thing. Seriously. You'll thank me."

"Not likely."

"You will."

"Piss off, Vergone."

I turn to leave him, to go back to my chaotic office and close the door, but he calls out to stop me. He isn't angry. Vergone is an economist, a theory man; he likes to speculate.

"What did you leave back there in Sicily, Joan?" he says. "Besides your mother, I mean?"

"Nothing," I tell him. "I was seven years old."

It's a continual bane to be thrown into the same hallway with Poli Sci men; they are such handsome, clever bastards.

But I write to Valparuta's *Commissione per l'avanzamento dei fondi culturali*, because Vergone really has done it to me this time.

It's a Roman feature writer's long, careless article, several months old, that Vergone puts in my mailbox. I wonder why he's giving it to me now. The clipping has been folded small, as if to fit an envelope, and then reopened. Vergone has pushed it into my box like this, without a note.

The Roman newsman's deprecating tone can't blunt the force of the story he tells. I read the whole thing through right there, in front of the faculty mailboxes. Popcorn is burning in the departmental secretary's electric popper; she's pinned behind her desk by a graduate student who lectures her in a voice of infinite patience, as if she were an imbecile. It's all ambience to me, negligible as light or air. I haven't thought about Sicily for years. It comes back to me now in shards, like most things buried for a long time, but the fragments are sharp as glass, whole as planets.

Gold-colored, crumbling Palermo. The narrow, squalid canyon that was our street in the Kalsa, the sudden gaps in its walls marked by old bomb craters debrided of rubble and left open, as if the vaporized buildings had been expected to grow back. A stone king entangled in a serpent, seated in a fountain's waters. My mother lighting a cigarette. The smell of developer.

I reach out, steady myself against the mailboxes' steel front. The ground shifts beneath me.

Weeks later, the *Commissione* replies: a blurred, eccentrically-worded brochure appears in my faculty mailbox, touting research opportunities newly available in Valparuta—a quaint walled city of some 1100 inhabitants, it says. I've never heard of it. A sketchy map locates it to the north and east of Trapani, just off the coast and well away from the Palermo-Trapani autostrada. I have no memory of the area, no certainty that I've ever been there. *These renowned archives,* the brochure reads, *revealed by earthquake decades ago, are now for the first time opened to scholars. A more complete record of Quattro-Settecento life in Sicily cannot be found. Scholars of Italian history and culture are encouraged to apply to the Programme for Visiting Scholars in care of the Commission for Cultural Resources.*

And then a collage of thumbnail images: a yellow Baroque edifice, canted against a sky whose color has defeated the brochure's printer; the patterned, undulating pavement of a vacant piazza; a view of distant sea.

And a tower.

If not for Vergone's newspaper clipping I would have thought it merely picturesque, a crenellated, gothic fortification set in a ruined keep. But I know what it is at once. It's the *rocca* where Valparuta's archives, hidden for centuries, appeared wholesale one day over thirty years ago, out of thin air.

That Roman feature writer had made a perfect hail of words of all that came down out of the tower's coffered floors: a mass of vellum-bound ledgers, incunabula in wooden boards, parchment documents scabbed with broken seals, packets of letters on good Sienese paper, cockled leather portfolios, trial balances, palimpsests, ordinances, credit notes, the scribes' chilblain rags, penknives and parings, vials of blotting sand and crusted ink, candle ends, saucer lamps— the list had gone on and on. Nothing had been lost in all that time, it seemed—except, perhaps, the breath of those who'd buried Valparuta's oldest municipal records in the tower's floors some two hundred and fifty years ago.

Certain other valuable lodes came to light in that earthquake, too: a sulfur deposit, a brisk thermal spring. Vergone's clipping said that in Calatafimi a Miocene beachhead appeared, the rim of an ancient lake where eccentrically-horned ungulates and early primates had died in numbers, leaving mineralized teeth, fragments of long bones.

Maybe Valparuta's *rocca*, too, had somehow entered the island's geology. Maybe it had become a formation of rock,

23

PITKIN COUNTY LIBRARY
120 NORTH MILL
ASPEN CO 81611

with fragments of history compressed in its strata. How else to account for the fall of books from its tower, the floors cracking open like earth overhead? How else to explain the archives' emergence with mineral beds and fossils?

But here is the difference.

If one of those Miocene deer had staggered up whole and living out of the Calatafimi shale, shaken the clay from its striped coat and trotted off to forage, then the reappearance of Valparuta's archives might have seemed less remarkable to me. But only then. And only then could I have stayed away, knowing that such a place of miracles could exist only in myth—that it would never be found on any map, in any country.

I apply to Valparuta's Programme for Visiting Scholars. For weeks I keep that flimsy brochure on my desk, letting its doubtful colors flame there amongst dreary term papers and committee minutes.

I am hoping daily for a fire.

CHAPTER THREE

I have my own office at Brown, a narrow cell off the foyer of the Macfarlane House, too near the door. It was a closet or a houseboy's cubby, I think, back when young men from good families did not dress or serve themselves. I'm glad to have it. The other lecturers share a big smoky bullpen in the departmental office upstairs—a wretched, convivial space.

Russell got the office for me. I didn't ask for it. I'd left four teaching posts in eight years, one just ahead of disciplinary action; I knew I wasn't suitable for academe. I'd left classes in shambles, freshmen in tears; I could only watch myself do these things. In American high school I'd struck books from tables, fought other girls in the bathrooms—the ones who'd regarded me archly, as if my defective speech and crippled grasp of American teen culture were a joke. Over time it seemed that I could only carry more and more down with me like a landslide, tentative friendships, second and third chances, all offers of sympathy.

Russell stood me on my feet this one last time, angrily, and I let him. That office in Macfarlane was meant to spare others, not me.

The Dean is doing me a favor, hiring you, Russell said. *Try not to embarrass me.*

You do the same, I told him.
It didn't work.

Even now, Russell generates receptions wherever he goes. Government agencies and archaeological societies will drag out buffet tables and call caterers and florists for his appearances; his reputation compels them. A photographer will be engaged and the press invited, mailing lists notified. There is no longer any burden upon Russell to live up to these preparations. The pressure to perform rests entirely upon his hosts. He is tirelessly gracious at these functions, and in his speeches he thanks no one.

But even before his career took off Russell was a formidable personality, I think, affable and deeply manipulative. Sicilians, who admire the art of appearance over the grubbing effort of achievement, would have appreciated this in him. At the outset of his first season of excavation at Morgantina, the *Associazione Archaeologica* in Aidone threw him a reception at the local museum. He met my mother there. He was thirty-five years old then—old as I am now—and was tenured faculty at Brown University's Center for Old World Archaeology. He had directed excavations in Greece and Calabria, published several key articles on the diffusion of obsidian along ancient Mediterranean trade routes. Among his crews he was known to be a womanizer; his female students jostled for his attention, brainless as goats. They should have known better than to encourage him.

I cannot conjure up my parents' meeting. I can imagine Quattrocento rooms and their contents, conversations centuries old, but not that first meeting of Simona Origo and Russell Severance. An image of Gorgon-headed antefixes on Plexiglas mounts, votive figurines and trays of antipasti stutters in my mind like a broken film and goes black— nothing else comes. I cannot put my mother and father in that room together, dressed and animated; I cannot make their eyes meet.

But somewhere early on in their tanglings I came along, a misjudgment, and after that one summer of excavation Russell never went back to Morgantina. He traded the site to Princeton, I think, for Solunto's ocean views and its safe distance from Aidone; my mother's family would have been obliged to injure him if he'd returned.

And Simona, willful and vindictive as any of those hayseed relatives of hers, took their bastard granddaughter and moved to Palermo for good.

I don't let anybody in my office. Not students, not colleagues. The walls are empty, there are drifts of papers on the floor. There are no reference books on the shelves, no runs of journals—just lists and lists in notebooks and binders, copies of old probates and inventories spilling out of bookcases onto the floor. I know it's all wrong, that the mess incriminates me. I can't amend it. It's out there like a premonition, crowded, aberrant; it has a meaning all its own, one that's still dark to me. It's not scholarship I'm doing anymore.

Vergone has seen my office. I let him in to put him off, but that didn't work, either; the world's a big mundane place to him, short on surprises. *So you're disorganized,* he said to me. *I thought you would be.* He'd taken it all in without concern.

But he asked me later, after the Faculty Disciplinary Committee had taken up my case and I'd been relieved of teaching, *How do you hold yourself together, Joan? You won't even help yourself—you've got the same mess here that's in your head.* He'd nudged a pile of notebooks with his toe.

He didn't seem to need an answer. But I saw something in his face that made me want to hit him, too: a kind of pained regret, as if he'd thought, until then, that I might still be salvaged.

She comes across the Commons at me, leaving the brick walk to the Student Union to head me off. I'm on my way to teach a section of Intro to Cultural Anth, and I'm late; there's a hard chilly wind off Narragansett Bay that smells of winter rain. It's one of those dull days, so short of light and purpose that nothing seems to matter. There are four sections of Anth 103, and they're interchangeable—four benumbed lecturers read the same notes in each class. The students catch a section like a bus and kill the time like commuters, reading books and newspapers, dozing off with their chins rocking on their chests.

I'd like to be the driver of that bus who loses it on purpose, who stands on the gas, yanks the wheel over and sends us all into a deep ravine at high speed, but that won't be today. I'm cold as a reptile, good for nothing.

She comes across the frost-killed grass at me with a stiff swing in her walk, lifting her hair away from her face— Andrea Eastman, a senior in the Classics department. She's expensively dressed down in black boot-cuts, cable-knit sweater and a factory-distressed bomber jacket. Her face says she's impatient with this pretense; she's done here with these college kids, she's left them all behind.

"Joan," she calls out. "Joan, I want to talk to you a minute."

She's got those long close thighs that make you think of statuary; she's had ballet and likely did the junior horse show circuit as a teen, riding a veteran hunter with more sense than she and beating the crap out of younger kids on ponies, then quitting before she had to go to amateur class and learn to lose.

I know all this because she's Russell's latest protégé. She's been in his old man's bed for six or eight months now, and it's going to her head.

"I hope you don't mind me telling you this," she says. She's put herself right in my face, so that I smell leather and designer perfume, her minty breath. "Your microhistory seminar? They're going to the Dean with a complaint."

"Are they," I say. It's taken them longer than I thought it would; they're a hangdog bunch, too easily demoralized.

"There's no syllabus," she tells me. "You come in un-prepared."

"Why are you telling me this, Andrea?"

"They thought you'd want to know—in case, you know, you want to try to do a better job."

"No, Andrea—why are *you* telling me this?"

For an instant she looks like what she is, a confused, spoiled girl. "Well, they asked me to!" she says.

"But you're not in the class," I say. "You're not a Student Advocate. Why would they ask you?"

Her mouth opens, closes. She's furious with me now for shaming her like this, for making her ridiculous. She thinks I've tricked her. She flushes violently, stares hard at some-thing in the distance—her receding dignity, perhaps. "You are so *not* what Brown is all about, Miss Severance," she tells me. "You are just a mean, bitter person."

"Get the fuck away from me, Andrea," I say.

"It's not my fault that nobody likes you. And I can't help it if Russell and I—"

She stops when she sees that I'm laughing at her.

"Andrea, he sleeps with all of you," I say. "Get away from me."

But now she has to even the score, never mind that she's got it totted up all wrong. If she knew anything she'd see that both of us are sorry planets, orbiting Russell's aging sun—and she by choice, at least. She's the less contemptible of us two.

But she bristles up; her voice climbs.

"He's sorry he got you a job here, did you know that?" she cries. "He told me he wishes he hadn't, that you're a mess and you're embarrassing him—"

I knock her down then. I do it like you'd choose a door to leave a room; I just pick a way out. I hit her in the face and she goes over on her tall shoes with a scream, more out of surprise than anything. I step over her; she's kicking like a foal, struggling to get up. People are angling over to her, walking sideways, not sure yet if it's any of their business.

I teach that canned Anth 103 lecture with verve, because I figure it's my last. It is.

A few weeks later Vergone puts that clipping in my mailbox.

Chapter Four

Chiesa leads me to the back of the reading room, under the marble staircase and down a dim vaulted passageway whose curved surfaces ring like bells as we pass. Away from the lobby's refaced walls and new doors the building is all rough pale stone, heavily buttressed, its constricted windows and doors deeply recessed. Scars from an old windlass and portcullis disfigure one arched doorway.

This was the old Spanish *bastillo*, Chiesa tells me—an armory and prison built at the end of the fifteenth century. "It makes a splendid library now," he says.

He stops at a low door, its threshold sunk below the level of the marble floor.

At first I think he's led me to a closet. The room is utterly black when he opens the door, and its air has the motionless, dense feel of a small space crammed full. But the room's smell—that faintly ammoniac odor of aged vellum, reminiscent of old urine—makes me slap the inside wall in search of the light switch.

The switch is on Chiesa's side. He reaches for it without haste.

The lights come on with a thump and a low fluorescent hum.

The room is no larger than a big parlor, and its windowless walls are of hand-dressed yellow limestone. It's an inner room, I realize, one with no outside wall. A suspended ceiling has been installed and hung with generous banks of lights; the carpeting is a pleasant green. New metal stacks fill the room, with hundreds of vellum-bound ledger-books ranged flat on their shelves in neat precision, stacked three or four high with their titled spines out. Flat and upright Hollinger boxes occupy the shelves at the back of the room, and one corner is given over to a small desk and computer station that must be Chiesa's. He's cleared the desk, perhaps for me.

I step down into the room and enter the stacks, and it's like going into a wash, an arroyo—except instead of bones and clasts protruding from its strata, whole worlds look out at me. Many of the books, I see, are bound in vellum scavenged from old antiphonals; their angular blackletter text and red musical notes lend the books a worn, harlequin air. Chiesa has wrapped severely cockled volumes in soft cloth tapes, running them head to tail and then spine to fore-edge and tying them off there, like a gift.

It's a spectacular treasure, this collection.

"Remarkable," I say aloud.

Chiesa answers from the other side of the stacks; he's shifting things on shelves. "Isn't it?" he says.

It was Chiesa who'd done the preliminary survey two years ago, Vergone's article had said. By then the collection had been locked in the library's crypt for nearly thirty years, thrown into cardboard boxes. No one had known exactly what those books and papers were.

Chiesa must have felt himself airborne, astounded, when he knew just what he had.

"The survey, that was your idea?" I call out to him. I'm touching crumpled spines, reading inked titles.

"Agretta was looking for items to market, things we had lying about," Chiesa's voice replies. "Our mongrel architecture, our vistas, this ambient backwardness of ours that passes for charm. He hadn't thought of the books from the tower. I suggested that they might be worth looking into."

He's downplaying his hard enterprise now, and I like it. "You took a chance," I say. "They might have been nothing— old bound newspapers and periodicals, that sort of thing."

"No," his voice says absently. "I knew."

And then he's standing at the head of the stacks, leaning there with a thick little book in one hand. "The earthquake's sound is what I remember, *Professoressa*—like a freight train running through the earth. But afterwards it was just a lark, no school for weeks, chickens running in the streets. We played all day in the broken water mains. No one bothered with the books in the tower. But when the winter rains came and the city had got back on its feet a bit, Baron Calabresi sent a group of us to gather them up, take them to the library. That huge mound of dirty, indecipherable writing— and such a strange pleasure, the feel of vellum between the fingers." He pushes himself upright, studies the morocco binding in his hands. "I think I always meant to come back to Valparuta to take charge of this collection," he says.

"You're a native, then." I hadn't known; Vergone's clipping had said only that he'd gone to university in Padua.

"I've been away a bit," he says.

Chiesa shows me the catalogue of the archives' holdings. It's a heavily-pencilled printout in a blue binder that he shows me with an air of impatience, as if he ought to have something better to show for his work. The pages' margins are filled with addenda and fierce-looking question marks—he's still modifying the collection's arrangement, he tells me. But he's hit upon a beautifully simple ordering system and documented it meticulously; Chiesa, I'm not too surprised to learn, is no plodding, hidebound listmaker.

He takes me through the catalogue page by page, series by series: Correspondence, Financial Records, *Fabbricaziòne*, the records of Valparuta's old *Infermeria*.

"Tell me again, *Professoressa*," he says. "What is it you're looking for?"

It's an innocent enough question—isn't it?—but I don't take it well. It's a problem I have, this feeling that everything shows on me, that no one is fooled.

"Probate records," I say. "Cargo lists, merchants' inventories. Did the *Commissione* not forward my application to you?"

"Of course they did," Chiesa says mildly. "But no one is quite themselves on applications, are they? No one says what they're really coming for."

He turns a few more pages. He has, I see, a conservator's spare, delicate manner of handling paper.

"I'm here for inventories, Signor Chiesa," I tell him.

"All right, then," he says. He smooths a page, sets a finger in the margin. "Here are what I've termed Municipal Notarial Records—a clumsy title, I'm afraid—but a very large series of ledger-books dating from 1380 to 1632. Your probate inventories are here. It's a good place to start, I think. Let me show you."

He leads me back into the archives, to a set of shelves stacked with books in scavenged vellum wrappers. I see a line of plainsong ornamenting one: *Beati quorum via.*

"May I, then?" I say to make him leave.

"Yes, of course," he says, but lingers.

I find what I want, a tall, worm-eaten volume in a stack of several others; the paper label on the shelf beneath it reads 1524–1526. I let the book fall open between my hands, and because this is a day of portents, the first entry I encounter is a probate record. I put my back to Chiesa.

He leaves me then, at last a bit put out.

Here's the thing about probates: you can revisit the homes of the dead.

They're lists of the possessions left in the homes of the recently deceased, recorded room by room, wall by wall. Probate officers—those who do this work—are time's own recordkeepers, a kind of geologic force; they're an unsparing lot, trading sentiment for rectitude. Every broken mattock, every soiled shirt and rush mat is recorded and assigned a value. Nothing escapes their notice. From probates you can reconstruct whole households like theater sets, put chairs against walls and baskets on pegs, you can set poultry in the yard.

In that application Chiesa saw I'd said that I planned to document levels of material wealth in sixteenth century Valparuta, that I wanted to study Renaissance furnishing patterns and storage strategies. Those weren't lies, exactly. They were more like a ring of keys to be tried on a door, one after the other, until the door opened.

I just wanted to get in.

This first inventory I've struck upon is brief and poignant, written in the racing hand of an official impatient to be gone. The deceased is an elderly widow, Giovanna Cipolla, who died one August morning nearly five hundred years ago. She owns nothing but scraps and castoffs, one old blanket and a single pot with a split rim. A distaff and a small bag of washed wool are listed just after her straw pallet.

I see the old woman bedridden, drawing out and twisting tufts of wool, catching fine new yarn up on her distaff. Her hands move like spiders casting webs. What used to be this woman's household has run quite away from her. It's filled now with a stranger's impolite children—her daughter-in-law's—and the house is out of order. Her son, uncertain in his mastery of his father's house, has set his mother in a corner where she won't see his mistakes. Outside, on Giovanna Cipolla's last morning, the summer sun seems like God's approaching glory, wrapped in a luminous cloak of dust.

I'm as bad as Chiesa, worse—I'm still standing in the stacks with my face in that first ledger-book when he speaks up behind me. I don't know how much time has passed.

"*Professoressa*," he says, "there's someone at the door." He's looking at me as if I've overslept.

And now I hear it, too, a steady, muffled pounding. It's been going on awhile.

"The door's locked?" I say stupidly.

"I didn't want us disturbed," he says.

He tells me then with an edge in his voice not to trouble myself, that he will look into this and return momentarily, but I follow him back out to the reading room anyway. I want to see who it is the archivist meant to keep from us. Chiesa turns back once to protest—he wants to seem a good host, anxious only to spare me this bother, but he can't locate the necessary phrases in the midst of all the pounding. It seems to go on and on. He throws me a look of mute reproach and hurries on.

It's a man at the library door, hammering away with a sort of patient industry—as if he were driving nails, not

36

looking to get in. He doesn't stop, even when Chiesa steps down into the vestibule with his keys. The archivist shoves the door open in the man's face and walks away, but the fellow pretends he's gotten the warmest of welcomes. He takes charge of the room with a small man's native swagger, looks around as if he's come to buy the place.

"Eh, Librarian," he shouts in guttural dialect. "You're supposed to be open! What are you up to in here?" He lets his eyes slide over to me.

He's a mechanic, I think, a tough little bantam in dirty blue coveralls—entirely unprepossessing except for this attitude he swings like a club. He's more dangerous than he looks. He has a handsome nose, a disfiguring scimitar of a chin, and his skin is bad, pitted with old acne scars. His right eye is glass, the original put out a long time ago and violently, I'd guess, given this hard jocose manner of his. Its gaze is fixed on some disconjugate middle distance, its color subtly wrong. The name patch on his coveralls reads *Nunzio* in loopy red embroidery.

Chiesa has gone behind the circulation desk and become, all at once, a government official. "There's nothing to be done about it, Signor Risacca," he says peremptorily, stamping due date cards. "I'll be in conference all afternoon—the mayor has seen fit to alter my schedule. Come back tomorrow."

The mechanic grins. "Agretta wouldn't let go of the *americana*, eh?"

"I said tomorrow," Chiesa says, but Risacca ignores him, settles himself for a visit, resting his forearms on a chair back.

"Well, Agretta thinks she's his, not yours," he says. "And why not? All that arm-twisting he did to get the *Commissione* to cough up the money for her, and of course he's always taking your women . . . oh, don't look like that, Chiesa! I don't mean it." He prowls around the room then, running a thumbnail over the tabletops, shifting books.

The archivist stares at him. "This is Signor Risacca, *Professoressa*," he says. "He repairs automobiles."

The mechanic makes his way over to me, bringing with him the smell of dirty machinery and solvent. "I have other skills, too," he says. "If you need a saint's intercession, for example—I can get it for you. If your neighbor has given you the evil eye, or you've got an important business deal—"

"You're a *mago*," I say.

He shrugs elaborately; it's not for him to say. "People come to me when they're worried," he says. "It makes them feel better."

I know his breed of swindler—men and women half-fooled themselves, thinking there might be something to those little plastic statues of Saint Joseph they bury in people's fields, the prayers written on slips of paper and burned—or chewed and swallowed—the trash fobbed off as charms dirtying people's pockets, staining their skin. They can't help their occasional faith, even if they took up the business for the money. They're a strange crew, folk healers one moment and confidence men the next; they steady themselves by charging outrageous fees.

It was the *maga* from via Pergole—an enterprising woman with three fat sons and no husband—who had set that basin of water on the floor in my mother's apartment and lit those candles. Her high, singsong incantations had sounded like children's ditties to me.

"This is a busy day for you," I say. "San Giovanni is cooperating?"

He looks me over, grinning. "I'm not telling, *ragazza*," he says. "That only gets me in trouble."

"With the saint? Or with your neighbors, after you've robbed them of their savings?"

In the silence I hear Chiesa's smothered laughter. Risacca's smile hardens.

"Are you sure this is the one you sent for, Chiesa?" he says. "She's not very agreeable."

"Oh yes," the archivist says, laughing. "She's the one."

"Be careful, Chiesa," the mechanic says. "Your shabby profession won't protect you—don't think that it will."

"What am I doing? What am I doing, besides my job?"

"You know what you're doing."

Risacca moves in closer to me then, too close, until I can hear his breathing. He's looking me hard in the face with his one good eye, the other reserving judgment. He wants me thinking right now of St. John the Baptist, and of truth divined from reflective surfaces. He's good, I realize; no doubt his neighbors fear him.

"There's something wrong with her, Chiesa," he says with casual authority, like a doctor reading x-rays. "She's not what you think."

I can't help it—I look at Chiesa. God knows what he sees on my face.

"Where did you find her?" Risacca says.

Chiesa stares at the book open under his hand. It has ugly, machine-printed endpapers, an inked-up card pocket. "Take the hocus-pocus outside, Risacca," he says. "She is who I think she is—I haven't made a mistake."

"Oh, sure, but she's not what you think. She's all fucked up."

Chiesa laughs a little, looks away. "That's the best you can do? 'All fucked up'?"

"She's not going to help you."

"She's not here to help me, Risacca. She's here to do research."

"She's not here to do either one, Librarian. I'm telling you—it's right there in her eyes. You could see it yourself if you wanted to."

He lets me go then, turns away. I want to shake myself, straighten my clothes. I feel like he's had me by the throat. Damn this place and what it's doing to me—I want to call his bluff but I can't get myself to do it. I think he might really know.

Chiesa's studying me as if I were a corrupted text.

"I shouldn't have let you in," he says, and for one freezing instant I think he's talking to me. But it's Risacca who answers.

"You can't keep me out," he says. "That's what I'm saying, Chiesa. None of this—" he gestures carelessly at the books, the room—"is going to protect you. So I'm telling you: be careful. You're not fooling anyone."

Chiesa stares at him, a long black look, and all that jesuitic calm of his is gone. He could kill the brutal little mechanic, I realize; he has it in him. Valparuta's archivist springs open and shut like a switchblade.

And I remember, as if it hasn't mattered until now, that he's a user—I've seen those dilated pupils of his.

"You've done your work here," Chiesa says hoarsely.

"Have I?" Risacca says brightly. "Then I guess I'll go. Not much of a job at all, really." He makes a great show of his satisfaction, throwing his shoulders back and gazing about with false benevolence. He turns to me. "*Professoressa,* no hard feelings, eh?" he says. "I can't help myself—I just say what I see. It's a tough gift I have, a kind of genius—!"

"Yes, I see that," I say. "Your gift is hard on everyone."

"Ah, don't be like that." He snaps his hand open like a magician, produces a cheaply-printed yellow card. "Here, I offer you my services—a palm reading, maybe—that's harmless enough, eh? Or if you should buy a car—Chiesa, you'd recommend me, wouldn't you? I'm a first-rate mechanic, aren't I?"

Chiesa nods stiffly. "He is."

"There, you see? He's an honest man! He wants to kill me, but he has to say it! There's no one better."

Chiesa stares determinedly at the books he's stacked on his desk. "Signor Risacca has a certain . . . rapport with cars, *Professoressa*," he says. "You'll never feel alone on the road again, with him as your mechanic."

I don't know what to say to this; it's all wrong, coming from the archivist. And then it's Risacca who moves to make some phony sense of it.

"Well, we all need a little watching over on the road, *Professoressa*," he says. "The roads are bad here, and our cars—well, you know. Our cars fall apart like women at a wedding."

I take the card from his outstretched fingers. Chiesa looks like something has slipped from his hands and broken on the floor.

Risacca, smiling, insults us both with little mincing bows. The door slams hard behind him.

Silence, except for tens of thousands of books breathing.

"You might have turned that down," Chiesa says to me.

"It's you who let him in," I say. "What did you do, lock the door just to piss him off?"

Chiesa shakes his head, makes an angry noise in his throat. We've shed the useful decorum of colleagues on short acquaintance and gone straight to close combat. This doesn't seem to concern either of us, angry as we are. For myself I feel as if I've taken off unnecessary gloves; I know Chiesa can take it.

I wonder if Risacca meant to shove me into the archivist like this, hoping for a fight and a break between us. He'll get his fight, I think.

"Do you usually let patrons overreach you like that?" I say. "Or was it the *mago* act?"

He trades a hot reply for one more barbed, more shrewd. "It seemed to work well enough on you," he says. He waits a moment, lets me note the score between us. "No, *Professoressa*, listen. Let me tell you something, eh? Risacca is . . . a close associate of the mayor's, do you understand me? He has Agretta's ear. Between them they demand a certain respect, because they can back up their claims, make people sorry. It's just the way it is. No one argues that the sky should not be blue . . . we live with it, it's not up for discussion. Do you see what I'm saying?"

He's looking at me with a kind of telegraphic urgency, wishing me to understand. Another old instinct comes back to me, dark as it was when I was ten, when smiles and easy words from strangers my mother encountered on the street could chill me.

Sicilian *omerta* isn't silence; it's a garrulous obliquity, a screen of euphemism. Agretta and the mechanic are *mafiosi*. I'm sure this is what the archivist is trying to tell me.

I suppose I could shout out, *Oh, you mean they're Mafia? They've got hold of you that way?* But it's like Risacca's *mago* act, it undoes me in an instant.

After Russell took me away that last time, my mother—freed of any thought for safety—spoke out endlessly against the Mafia, in interviews, at rallies, extempore on the street. I stumbled over news of Simona Origo as I hacked my way through American high school, came across snatches of her overwrought diatribes, delivered like epic poetry: *our beautiful struggle*, she said again and again. *We throng the streets, arm in arm, joyfully, singing powerful words against the Mafia.*

She hurt her cause, I think.

The *Palermitani* followed her like a soap opera. She made such passionate theatre of their sorry lives, let them think they were heroes just for wearing sloganed T-shirts and emoting in numbers in the street. And all the while prosecutors, judges, chief inspectors kept on dying. It was she who'd photograph them then—half-buried in bombed courtyards, sprawled in bullet-riddled cars—and see her photos published in the papers for another round of tardy, self-serving public outcry.

She should have ridden the *Palermitani* like a harridan, called them ninnies, weaklings, collaborators. She should have told them to go get their guns and knives and clubs, their ropes and fists, and kill the made men any way they could. *They are rats, snakes,* she should have said, *and you are timid fools. Crush their heads, burn their bodies.*

In the end the *Palermitani* did get ugly, of course—but by turning on my mother, not the Mafia. She shouldn't have gotten in the car with that prosecutor, they said. Everyone knew Leoluca Dandi was a dead man after the indictments he'd brought down. Why did she go with him? The talk grew darker, coarser; editorials recalled that Simona Origo had never married, that she'd been seen over the years in the company of many men.

What was she doing in that car with him?

A rumor surfaced finally, an off-color joke that was choked off, that caused fierce hilarity: *She'd had her head in his lap!* it said.

Chiesa heads back toward the archives without a word. We're less happy with each other now, less happy with ourselves; it's the mechanic's doing. Someone watching us might think we've brushed aside his interruption, dismissed it and gone back to work, but in fact Risacca's got us backtracking, hunting after something that we've lost.

This is how spells work, how voodoo, prayers and prophesies take hold. A clever one drops a stone into deep water, and we are rocked—not by the stone but by our own fears, our underwater secrets. He's done his work on both of us; the ripples are travelling outward.

What did that girl feel at seeing armies in a pan of water, soldiers where her future husband should have been? What was at the heart of her surprise, I wonder? Was it that she saw anything there at all, or was she ready for a man's face? Or was it, finally, the shock of recognition as she saw her inner army, the population of her darker fancies?

CHAPTER FIVE

So I occupy Valparuta like it's a cheap hotel room, a place to be when the archives aren't open, to eat and sleep. It's all familiar to me, the rubble walls and faded stucco, the mingled smells of trash and food, the compact, overly-demonstrative people who work to make your business theirs. The effects of St. John's Day have passed, and I'm back in a place I know too well to like.

It's no great surprise, I tell myself, that I had Sicily's measure when I was ten, or that my estimate of it still stands twenty-five years later. There's a stubborn rusticism here that whittles everything down, that willfully defeats itself; there's sophistication only in the way small-mindedness is practiced. A child can make sense of it. Valparuta is just like Palermo and Aidone were then. It wearies me, the sameness.

So I spend days poring over the inventory of a minor noble's cluttered household, revisiting the crowded chambers of a fine country villa that's been gone for centuries now. The dead baron's large family hovers just out of view, nephews and a favored youngest son, a second wife, a widowed sister, the family retainer on whom they all depend. They stand behind screens and doors with their hands in their sleeves, anxious, acquisitive. They leave rooms ahead of the probate

45

official, stirring the tapestries in their haste so that the house seems haunted, though the old baron has departed his family's thoughts entirely. The house is crammed with furniture, linens, rugs, crockery, glass, statuary, books. The women whisper among themselves; the men keep their counsel. The retainer speaks to the sons in a language of feudal deference that somehow elevates him above his masters, greeting them *I bow to you, I kiss your hand*. He can ruin them if he chooses. It's his ilk—the shrewd managers of a profligate aristocracy's estates—who will offer their frightened employers protection for a price in later years, and then become the Mafia.

The days are hot and uniform, like a closed room. There's nowhere to go. Long scarves of acrid, unbreathable air wind through the city, spangled with ash. It's just farmers burning the spent wheatfields below Valparuta, readying them for October's planting, but up here in this blind, walled city it's as if we're under siege. I imagine armies crossing the fields below, burning everything in their path.

There will be no rain for months now.

Valparuta's Commission for Cultural Resources has put me up in a small suite of rooms at the Elimo, the city's only three-star hotel. It's an extravagant gesture, something a failing enterprise might do to prop up confidence, to hide its desperation. If it mattered to me I might worry about Valparuta giving its amenities away like a dying relative, but it doesn't. Neither of us are what we say we are.

The Elimo is an old hotel, and it has some mild pretensions. Its walls are hung with paintings in deep gilded frames, brown landscapes and gaudy genre paintings of Greco-Roman feasts. A great bronze greyhound sits in an alcove, an expression of rudimentary knowledge on its face. And there's a tall old museum case in the lobby, big as a cupboard, filled with worn figurines, glass unguentaria and a fine Attic black-figured krater—grave goods pilfered, I suspect, from a nearby Greek necropolis. I stop to admire them, to bemoan them, every time I enter the hotel. The desk clerk, a self-possessed young woman whose still, sharp-featured face is nearly beautiful, greets me with a queen's detached amusement. *Good evening, Professoressa,* she says. *All is as you left it—I've been watching them for you.*

Russell would enjoy this display of contraband, set out like an old cabinet of curiosities. He has a pothunter's impulse to take things, to please himself—and he would be reminded, I think, of the tiny *Museo Archeologica* in Aidone, where he first met my mother, where he first exercised a minor celebrity's capricious will.

I smile at the desk clerk; she smiles back minutely. We're friends.

Piero Quagliata is the one who changes everything.

I've been working for three hours on a Wednesday morning when I meet him. I'm on that middle passage across the day and through the week, plowing a sea of old documents and out of sight of landfall. You let go of things in mid-passage. It's my second or third week in Valparuta, I'm not sure which. Chiesa visits the archives dependably like a seventh wave, on business of his own. He touches the edge of my desk as he passes.

Piero Quagliata comes up like a fog.

He dies suddenly in 1552, on the Thursday of the Christmas Ember Season, three weeks into Advent. He's a youngish man, married but childless, a weaver. He leaves his distraught wife with a house full of tablecloths and a half-woven warp on his loom. Death is a common visitor to households at this time, lives are short—but Piero's abrupt passing defies all remaining expectations. He isn't sick, he's neither young nor old; his lungs and heart are sound. He goes to bed fasting on Thursday evening as the season requires, tossing a bit, perhaps, restless with hunger and impatient with the early dark. But he's a blameless man of modest fortune and good work habits; he falls asleep. His wife wakes in the morning to find her husband dead beside her.

The probate officer is at pains to stress the timing of Piero's death. In his words I hear the long anxious journey the faithful took each winter then, down through darkening days toward salvation and rebirth—an ancient, perilous passage from the old year to the new. The official is shaken, much moved; his writing slants downward toward melancholy, he scratches out words. Piero leaves one good chair with carved arms and an embossed leather seat, myriad wooden kitchen implements, a six-harness loom so massive it stands in a room all its own, a painted floorcloth. The official records it all in indiscriminate detail. He's looking for answers, for a sign of God's purposeful hand.

Piero's bereaved wife impedes his work.

The widow Quagliata, greatly distressed, has summoned three workmen against my wishes, the official scrawls in a margin. *She urges them to remove the roof of the house without delay, though my work is not yet finished.*

I see the poor woman weeping, dishevelled, keening about the house. The workmen regard her dumbly; their hands hang at their sides, clutching tools of no use to them here. They need wings made of balsawood, wax and feathers; they need a theater crane and its wires to fly them out of this appalling scene. The widow shrieks at them, begs them to tear off the roof—her dead husband's soul is trapped in the house, she says, blundering against the windows like a bird. It's work they've done often, that's not the problem; their friends will do the same for them when they die, ignoring, like emergency workers, the local priest's disapproving scowl.

But this time the workmen stand like oxen, insisting in low voices that they will not take the widow's money, they will not remove the roof. They know nothing of gentle persuasion, of how to make her understand. All they know to do is measure out their strength against a job and set about it. They tell her again and again in the same words, the same tone, that her husband's soul is not in the house. It isn't here, Signora, they say. It isn't here. It isn't here. The widow tears her hair, screams, beats herself against their stolid bewilderment.

It's the probate officer who steps between them, demanding an explanation.

These men claim to be benandanti, *and friends of the deceased,* he writes. *They fear reprisal and so speak to me in confidence, though surely what they tell me is madness. Piero Quagliata, they say, went out with them in spirit on Ember Thursday in defense of the planted wheat, leaving his body behind; his soul failed to return by cockcrow and so was lost abroad. With great conviction they assure me of this. The roof should stay in place, they say, and masses bought instead to pray for the weaver's wandering soul.*

And that's all.

I study the words like they're tea leaves but there's nothing behind them, nothing in their shape to tell me how this ended. The official is in difficulty, certainly, like a man who's fallen in a goat pen; all around him is the stink of superstition, and agitated creatures unmindful of his clothes. He's anxious for his long lace cuffs, and for his soul. He wants to keep his distance—if only he were not so needful of a purposeful world, if only the workmen's whispered claims had not struck him so hard.

He's heard of these *benandanti*. He's heard about this business they attend to on Ember Thursday nights, the parting of souls from bodies.

What he doesn't see is that at times like this, when God has hidden His face from him, he falters toward belief in such things himself.

I show the entry to Chiesa.

He's on his way into the stacks again when I stop him. He's been in and out of them all morning, carrying volumes bound in wooden boards and tawed pigskin, or got up handsomely in blind-tooled crimson calf. He's working on a descriptive index of bindings, he's told me—something he turns to when he's feeling restless, when he's no good for anything else.

His pupils are contracted today, and he's lost that look of a man who can see in the dark. It's diminished him, going without whatever he's been on. He's crabbed and impatient, older, thinner. He's trying to do without, maybe, to show himself that he can still work when he's straight, but he's proving himself wrong.

He raps the pages that I show him with his knuckles, pushes the ledger-book back into my hands. "You haven't run across this sort of thing?" he says. "In all those studies of yours?"

"Have you?"

He shrugs, puts his fingers in the small of his back and stretches, grimacing. He's having muscle aches, maybe spasms; he's in mild withdrawal.

"Have you?" I ask again.

"Well, they're not exactly unprecedented, these references to folk beliefs," he says. "You know that."

"But going out in spirit in defense of the crops? And this fear of reprisals? What were these *benandanti*, a secret society of some kind?"

Chiesa is trying very hard to attend to me, to honor my questions, but he's having trouble. He laughs a little, turns away with his hands in the air, as if it's me who's done him in and not his strung-out nerves. "You ask so many questions!" he says.

"I'm curious, that's all," I say, but that's not quite true either.

"These *benandanti*—" he says, and stops. He's forgotten what he meant to say, or remembered something else. He seems to be reading empty air, a difficult translation; his lips are moving.

I wait for him like he's my slow-witted brother, in need of some forbearance.

"They weren't a sect of any kind, really," he says at last. "By the late seventeenth century all sorts of half-baked ecstatics and swindlers were calling themselves *benandanti*, *Professoressa*—epileptics and fake mediums, women who swore they could visit the dead and locate lost objects. It's not a useful term."

"But this agrarian variant is earlier than that," I say. "Have you heard of it before?"

"I don't know, *Professoressa*. I—"

He stops again. He's trying to contain his agitation but he can't, not entirely. I've heard that jonesing addicts sometimes try to shed their uncomfortable skins like snakes; the clothes come off, the scratching begins. Chiesa's not there yet, but he might be seeing it in his future.

The only help I can offer is distraction, and for his dignity the pretense of a blind eye. "It's the remnant of a fertility cult, don't you think?" I say. "A carryover from pre-Christian times."

He laughs strangely. "I suppose it could be," he says. "My point is that it wasn't a distinct tradition—not historically, at least. You can't subject it to proper study; it has too many errant meanings. It's like trying to study people who say they are 'helpful' or 'intrepid'—you just can't."

But it's out of character, this pessimism of his. I know Chiesa too well already to be fooled. For weeks now he's scoured the archives' shelves as if my dull work were his passion, found me records of old sumptuary laws, joiners' account books, treatises on domestic life. He's leaned in over the knotty, colorful bits of Castilian argot I've found, grinning like a kid crowding a peephole; he's tracked down tithing lists, tax rolls, church records. Nothing defeats him. The tangles and lacunae of history are delicious to him—he chews through them like pasta, in great mouthfuls. Even sick he'd never refuse a tasty problem like this one. This is too much of a hard sell I'm getting from him.

"So you'd discourage pursuit of the subject," I say.

"I—no, not *discourage, Professoressa*," he says. "I'd only warn you—that you'd be wasting your time."

"You're warning me?"

He gives me a black look that wavers away.

"You've been warned about this, too," I say. "Haven't you."

He freezes. Chiesa has this heron's instinct when a nerve's been touched and he fears giving too much away; I've seen it before. He watches me down the high slope of his nose like a bird in reeds.

"Have you been directed to restrict my access to the collection?" I say. "Tell me you haven't."

He doesn't deign to answer me directly. Instead he seems to listen for a moment, his gaze turned inward. When he moves again it's as if his stillness has been of no consequence. It's the strangest thing to watch him step out of hiding, his measured movements. He pulls a hand through his hair, turns casually into the stacks.

"Of course, *Professoressa*, if you're determined to misuse your time in this way, that's entirely your choice. I'll assist you if I can."

"And can you?"

He's disappeared into the stacks; his indifferent voice comes back to me. "Where do you suppose we might begin to look?" he says.

I consider this. Folk beliefs are the province of the unlettered, those who hold them don't write them down. It's only when folk draw the notice of the law or the Church—when their beliefs jerk them like puppets and they are deemed mad, obstinate or victims of the Devil—that a record sometimes survives.

And the officials never get these matters right, either, no matter how many times the peasants, the goatherds, the housewives explain the workings of their world.

"Rome might have taken a hard look at these *benandanti*," I say.

"Well, yes, if anyone of consequence bothered to denounce them," Chiesa's bleak voice replies. "The Holy Office had lost interest in these clumsy anomalies by then, you know. The Church had bigger fish to fry—Lutherans, bona fide witches—"

53

I can't help it; I burst out laughing. "Are there any Inquisitorial records in your holdings, Signor Chiesa?" I say.

Silence. I hear him sigh, I hear a quick whisper of fabric. When he speaks his voice is strangely muffled. "You know where the catalogue is," he says.

If I didn't know better I'd say that out of my sight he'd put his elbows on a bookshelf—that sound of clothing—and buried his head in his arms.

CHAPTER SIX

It's a strangely unedited entry that I find in the catalogue, a line of words left untouched in the midst of all Chiesa's redlined text and scribbled margins. *Inquisitorial Records*, it says. *1 box containing 3 folders.* And a shelf number.

Chiesa has left the archives again without speaking to me, carrying books for his binding project. I don't think he's going to get much done, for all his show of industry. I can smell his illness on him now, a sour odor like an adrenaline sweat.

His silence is a protest, maybe, or just a symptom of his misery. It isn't meant to deter me. He surely knows by now that he can't—that I'll just hunt him out if I have questions. I don't care if he disapproves of what I'm doing.

I'm just curious about this weaver's death, I tell myself— and since I've ditched my career like a stolen car it doesn't matter what I do. I could even leave Valparuta, I suppose, embarrass Chiesa and blow town; I could rent a dingy hotel room in Mondello and spend the days on the beach in my streetclothes like a Moroccan, eating greasy *arancini* out of waxed paper. I'm just killing time, really—the weeks and months it's going to take for the University to dig me out like a thorn, for Russell to dissociate himself from my unruliness.

But I don't want to sit on the beach in the sun's hot, indiscriminate bath. I want to pry the secrets from those three tight-lipped *benandanti*, know the source of their peculiar authority, their burdensome visions. There's illumination and then there's illumination; the truth is that sunlight hurts my eyes.

Chiesa, with his secret vice, would understand.

But the narrow, upright box I take from the shelf is too light, the three folders inside too slender to hold much of use. They're just public abjurations, three long dull renunciations of the odd behavior, superstition and gossip that inquisitors sometimes took for heresy. The town crier had bawled these disavowals out in church over the heads of their three mute penitents, who probably couldn't have read them anyway.

There's no mention of *benandanti*.

Something isn't right, though. Dissatisfied, I shake the box a little, listen to the thin folders shift inside. The same inquisitor had put his hand, his seal to each of these abjurations—a most reverend lord Girolamo Puglisi, vicar general and apostolic commissioner of the diocese. This powerful prelate had come all the way from Palermo; the trials' scattered dates suggest that he must have returned to Valparuta at odd intervals over nearly twelve years to pursue these trivial cases.

Why would he have bothered? Better yet, why would Rome have instructed him to do so? There's a half-witted woman who supposedly ate meat on Fridays and bewitched her neighbor's child; there's a harmless blowhard accused of freethinking, a midwife who had put charms in her client's bed. Negligible stuff, all of it, even by late sixteenth century standards. It doesn't make sense.

Unless the inquisitor was already in town at those times.
On other, more serious business.

I flip the box open again, stare at the inquisitor's tall signature, the cluttered heraldry of his seal. His thoughts might have been elsewhere when he put his name to these documents. The way we sign for cash received, maybe, while we think about the balance.

I pull my fingers over the folders' tops once more, just for the card's soft snap and the smell of old wax. And that's when I see it: something's been written in pencil well down on the inside of the narrow box. Even upside-down I recognize Chiesa's hand. I turn the box around, tip it toward me. *Confessions 163*, it reads.

For the next two days I seem to put my hand on matters hidden from me until now. I can find no entries for confessions of any sort in the catalogue, no box or length of shelf numbered 163, but out on the street I walk right into surprising finds. They could have been there all along, these incidents, beneath my notice; they could just be coming to the surface now. I'm not sure. I remember walking surface surveys with Russell near Pantalica, the things he could see on the ground that were invisible to me and his green, admiring crew. He knew what he might find there, and so he found it: a bronze fibula, tesserae, fossilized bone, tiny lumps of Byzantine glass. You'd swear he'd planted the stuff himself the night before, he shopped the ground so easily for artifacts. I suspect myself of the same thing now, manufactured discoveries that let me claim surprise like a greenhorn.

And that ridiculous code grates on me. I won't let it be anything else, not an errant doodle or a jotted reminder of something unrelated. Chiesa is playing cloak-and-dagger with the collection, hiding things from researchers—from me. He's more capable of this than he is of carelessness, I know it.

These are the things I see:

A well-dressed businessman pissing on a colleague's car—after embracing the man fondly and watching him walk out of sight. It's late morning on a street of shops; a dozen witnesses glance toward the bright yellow arc and the miniature sound of rain as if checking their reflections in a window.

A man approaches me on the street, smiling like a dog. He has broken away from a knot of his accomplices who are struggling to tip a barrowload of patio bricks into the street. Several men stand with their backs to the barrow, shielding the action, on the lookout for witnesses. I've left the library for a *caffè* out of disgust; in all of Chiesa's finding aids, catalogue appendices and manuals I can find no mention of confessions, nothing numbered 163.

The man holds me there in the street, one hot hand gripping my elbow. "These bricks, *Professoressa*," he says confidentially. "They're better off so, eh? It's a favor we're doing." He touches a finger to his cheek, tugs his eyelid down.

"*Strónzo!* Pervert! Let go of me," I shout in my hoarsest, best Sicilian. "My brother will kill you."

But the man just laughs, puts his hands behind his back. "No, no, *Professoressa*, it's no good," he says, wagging his head. "You see, we know it's you. But you don't know anything about bricks, now, do you? Anything about how they sometimes come to lie in the street like this?"

I tell him to get out of my way. Somehow that's enough to satisfy him; he backs away from me, grinning. "Tell Chiesa you saw Sostene hard at work," he says. "Tell him Sostene sends him greetings."

After this it seems there's wreckage everywhere. I see a ceramic planter shattered against a doorstep, starred windowpanes, fresh laundry scattered over a courtyard. This isn't the work of *mafiosi*. It's too petty, too widespread; it seems that everyone in Valparuta has taken sides. I pass Sostene's message on to Chiesa just to find out what it means.

"We have a long history together, Sostene and I," Chiesa tells me. He's sharpening a pencil down to nothing.

"You're friends, then."

"I know him, *Professoressa*. He's not my friend."

All at once I see it, what he means. The fat *maga* would say that my third eye has opened. "Like you know the mayor. Like that," I say.

I hear the pencil's lead snap off inside the sharpener's body. Chiesa begins grinding it down again. "Yes," he says. "Like that."

I don't ask him about the code written in the box. Something else has occurred to me—something I should have noticed at once.

Chiesa wrote *Confessions* there, not *Confessioni*—he wrote it in English.

It's a title, or part of one. And 163, then, must be a page number.

So I search the library's old card catalogue, a huge mahogany chest on bulbous Empire legs that fronts the Reference section. It's like returning to the elegant old gentleman who first seduced you as a girl, going back to a card catalogue.

Its smell, its genteel workings still stir you like no searchable database can. The cards are going brown on their edges; they've been rolled into a manual typewriter, typed laboriously, and corrected by hand. There's a story to each. You hook your finger in each drawer's brass pull and it slides out with a pleasurable groan.

I hear Chiesa behind me at the circulation desk, rustling papers, clearing his throat. He's watching me.

I thumb through the title cards. There are only a few in English, a motley collection that likely came to the library by chance, one by one, like stray dogs. Edward Henry Smith's *Confessions of a Confidence Man*. Schoenberner's *Confessions of a European Intellectual*. An English edition of *The Confessions of Jean-Jacques Rousseau*.

And, incredibly, what must be a first edition of Thomas de Quincey's *Confessions of an English Opium-Eater*. It's a London imprint, dated 1822.

I nearly laugh out loud, it's so perfect: Chiesa's secret cross-reference is a title both self-referential and self-deprecating—and one that shows off the library's holdings, too. Behind me Chiesa has begun rifling his desk drawers, opening and closing them one after the other.

The title card sends me back to the archives, to a shelf stacked with rare books in custom-made Solander boxes. I should be wondering where Chiesa has found the money to house his books this way—there's something incriminating in the achievement, I swear, dazzled *commissione* or no—but I've found de Quincey's extravagant, tortured memoir. It's a fat little octavo volume bound in carmine half-leather and swirling paste-grain; its edges are marbled. I page through it quickly, forcing myself to take proper care. The pages are barely foxed, the book's been cut down only once; it's an original binding.

I arrive in the midst of de Quincey's nightmarish with-drawals. He's trying to cut back his dose but he can't, the poppy's in his blood; he enjoys a few days of euphoria but then his body begins to scream. He's turned his relentless, transcendent vision inward, taken himself apart like a watchworks and discovered himself to be jewelled, intricate, beautiful, utterly debased. He's never had an unconscious moment, it seems. He's never forgotten anything. He's a child at night again, in withdrawal; he's returned to the bright hypnagogic imagery of waking dreams. Vast processions, buildings, dances, battles pass before him in the darkness, just as they did when he was a boy; their insufferable splendor frets his heart.

I turn to page 163. There's a tiny pencilled checkmark in the margin.

Many years ago, I read, *when I was looking over Piranesi's* Antiquities of Rome, *Mr Coleridge, who was standing by, described to me a set of plates by that artist, called his Dreams, and which record the scenery of his own visions during the delirium of a fever. Some of them (I describe only from memory of Mr Coleridge's account) represented vast Gothic halls: on the floor of which stood all sorts of engines and machinery, wheels, cables, pulleys, levers, catapults, &c. &c. expressive of enormous power put forth and resistance overcome.*

No, I think, de Quincey's unnatural memory has failed him here—those etchings of Piranesi's weren't called *Dreams*. Not *Sogni*, not *Illusioni*—something else. But it escapes me now. I can see those giant shadowed dungeons, though, their bizarre accumulation of ornament and object, vaults and arches, drawbridges, smoking pyres, grotesque friezes, chains, gallows, spoils of war . . . They're famous images, you can find them in almost any library, lurking like sudden hallucinations among the art books on the Oversized shelves. And like Mr. Coleridge, you never forget Piranesi's vast, claustrophobic halls once you've seen them.

But I've lost what they were called. I run up against titles of individual plates in my mind but they're like walls, I can't get past them: *The Grand Piazza. The Pier with Chains. The Staircase with Trophies. Prisoners on a Projecting Platform.*

I close the little book on my finger, stand looking sourly at nothing.

Because it's a trick. Chiesa has tricked me.

He's sent me around in a circle, out from himself and then back; the title of those famous plates won't tell me anything. Chiesa is the only one who knows the significance of this passage, what it has to do with that box of Inquisitorial records. That's the message here: *You must go through me.*

And he's right here, I discover—Chiesa's located himself here on the page, trapped in Piranesi's endless labyrinths:

Creeping along the sides of the walls, de Quincey continues, *you perceive a staircase: and upon it, groping his way upwards, is Piranesi himself: follow the stairs a little further, and you perceive it come to a sudden abrupt termination, without any balustrade, and allowing no step onward to him who has reached the extremity, except into the depths below. Whatever is to become of poor Piranesi? You suppose, at least, that his labours must in some way terminate here. But raise your eyes, and behold a second flight of stairs still higher: on which again Piranesi is perceived, but this time standing on the very brink of the abyss . . .*

It's him; of course it is. But what is it about those meager trial records that leads Chiesa to see himself on that staircase?

I slip de Quincey's book back into its box, return it to the shelf. And as if on cue the archivist appears, sweating, distracted, carrying a stack of books between his hands like a cake. He stops in the doorway.

"You have a first edition of de Quincey's *Confessions,*" I call out to him, and watch him flinch. After a moment's hesitation he joins me in the stacks, busies himself with shelving.

"Yes, the de Quincey," he says. "A ridiculous thing for a municipal library to hold. I should sell it, of course—buy a set of encyclopedias, something the schoolchildren could use."

"I don't know," I say. "I think you should keep it. There's no shortage of funding here."

I'm leaning against those shelves of custom-made boxes. Chiesa takes a breath to contradict me, maybe, or put me in my place—but he bites back his words.

I brush by him on my way out of the archives. "Ask the *Commissione* for the funds to purchase the encyclopedias," I say. "Ask the mayor."

I just want to piss him off, see if he'll let something slip. But my own brutality makes me wince: there's that tiny, attenuated figure, climbing stairs to nowhere.

Whatever is to become of poor Piranesi?

One last, surprising revelation while I'm worrying this business of the *benandanti*:

I'm in the *drogheria* near the hotel, and it's evening. I'm looking for something in a shapely bottle that will drench me like a bucket pulled up from a well, that will wash my skin of this pervasive dust. The *drogheria* is hot and dim, full of the odors of liniment and face powder.

Back among the toiletries there's a woman lifting bars of milled soap to her nose. I'm not pleased to share the space with her. But she's not the usual Sicilian housewife, kitchen-bound and gaining weight, imperious in stores. She looks like she could still break into a run like a girl, her height and long legs carrying her past all her friends. She has a heavy gold wedding band on her finger but still wears her dark hair long—asking for trouble, I think. But then, watching her, I think that she may have some form of immunity. There's no watchfulness in her. She makes room for me; I've joined her, it seems.

We pick the shelves together like prospectors.

The woman sighs. "They're all too French, these soaps," she says. "I'd smell like a vase of flowers—what an injustice!" We share the joke for a moment, discreetly, and then she leans into me. "Chiesa isn't eating well, *Professoressa*—I see it. I'm concerned for him," she says under her breath. "Can you encourage him to take a bit more?"

A moped howls by outside like a buzzsaw run down the street. "I'm afraid you're mistaken, Signora," I tell her. "The archivist and I are not close friends."

She chooses not to hear this. "He has his library," she says. "He should be happy, happy—no one begrudges him that. Please tell him for me."

"I'm Chiesa's colleague, Signora. We are not friends."

"But you see him, don't you? You see that he's ill. Say something to him, won't you?"

"What should I say, Signora?"

She finds me as useless, as laughable as the French soaps. "Remind him that this was what he wanted, *Professoressa*," she says at last.

The clerk leans over the counter like a suitor as she goes out the door. "Good evening, Signora Agretta!" he says ardently in her wake.

She's Agretta's wife.

I stumble back to the hotel in incomplete darkness. A big moon has risen early, throwing double shadows; people trail faint twin shades of themselves down the street. I put my feet down where the cobbles seem to be but they're deeper than I think, the half-dark refracting like water, and I'm sure again and again that I'll fall.

The Elimo's lobby is all candid surface, discreetly lit. The desk clerk nods to me, returns to the fashion magazine she's opened out before her. She might be reading the mahogany desk's grain like hieroglyphs, her chin in her hands.

The light adds my reflection to the contents of the big museum case.

And then Chiesa pushes through the hotel door, still in his good dark suit. He's carrying a white plastic shopping bag that's weighted at the bottom. He's neither surprised nor pleased to see me.

"*Buona sera, Professoressa,*" he says, warning me away. He strides across the lobby's river of balding Brussels carpet and takes the stairs two at a time.

The desk clerk returns to her study.

"Signorina," I say. "Where is Signor Chiesa going?"

She looks up, folds the backs of her hands against her throat. She's thinking of sling-backed heels, a watered silk cocktail dress. "To his rooms, *Professoressa,*" she says. Her tone tells me that I should already know this. "I look the other way when he brings in food," she whispers. "Don't tell anyone."

I smell it now, *girarrosto* chicken and onions incubating in a foil-lined bag. It's just the thing for Chiesa's sour stomach. You could be near death, stuffed full, sick as a dog and you'd still want to bolt a *girarrosto*, pick the carcass with your fingers.

"The archivist lives here?" I say.

She gives me a look of polite scorn. "Yes, of course. All the way up," she says, drawing the magazine's limp, glossy pages aside one by one. "It's still in the old style up there, very elegant—but it hasn't been kept up. I wouldn't live there, myself. I would have demanded an apartment in via Rabata—it's more fashionable."

I pretend to study the *ristorante* menu on the desk. "Has Signor Chiesa lived here long?" I ask.

The desk clerk shrugs. "Two years, I think—a little more. It was before my time."

"What a fine thing, to be able to say where one wishes to live."

"I would have done better, *Professoressa*. He could have lived anywhere; the mayor would have given him any place he wanted." She contemplates a handbag in an angry-looking model's hand. "He's beginning to regret his choice, I think."

"Oh?"

"He stays away. I don't see him in the lobby, and when I go home at night there are lights on in the library. And he's started to say things about his rooms."

"What does he say?"

The desk clerk turns her gaze from the handbag to me. Her expression doesn't change. "He says they are his *carcere*—his prison. In his mind."

And again that third eye of mine starts wide open.

"He calls his rooms his *carcere d'invenzione*," I say.

"Yes, that's it—his imaginary prison. He laughs when he says it, of course, but I don't think he's joking."

He's not. Because those etchings of Piranesi's, those black vaults where the archivist sees himself climbing stairs forever—they're called *Carceri d'Invenzione*.

Imaginary prisons.

Chapter Seven

I follow Chiesa up the stairs.

The Elimo's top floor likely hasn't seen guests in thirty years. In the hallway the old light fixtures and their glass globes—opaque as jellyfish—have been converted to electric, but nothing's been done since; iron water-pipes have been punched through corners from floor to ceiling and the damage left unrepaired. Salon doors in old green paint stand open onto tall suites of rooms full of derelict furniture and splintered rafts of carved oak panelling. The floors are tiled in green and white marble, blackening at their edges.

Chiesa's rooms are at the end of the hall, facing away from the street. The doors there have been cleaned and a new lock installed. There's no sound from inside.

I knock once and wait. There's a long silence, as if the rooms are empty, but when I finally hear movement inside the door opens almost immediately. He's been standing at the door the whole time, waiting for me.

"Good evening, *Professoressa*," he says again. I'm not to presume that he's the same man who spoke to me downstairs—and in fact he's not the same. His jagged edges are gone, and in their place there's this elevated calm that's just a little too flat, too engineered. And he's changed his clothes, tucked his crumpled, day-old dress shirt into faded jeans; he looks good in them, cowboy-thin as he is. He's pushed his bare feet into a pair of old scuffs.

"Good evening, Signor Chiesa," I say. "Have I found the archives' off-site storage?"

He's loose enough to enjoy the joke. "There's no such thing, of course," he says. "Come in."

His rooms are bare as a beach cave, scoured clean. He hasn't painted or replastered; cracks travel down the ocher-colored walls. The windows' wooden casements and shutters, the tall doors are all the color of buckeyes. The room is filled with dark yellow light, a permanent sundown.

Chiesa leaves me, goes through a narrow doorway to the kitchen. "Have you dined, *Professoressa*?" he calls out to me. "No? An *aperitivo*, then." He returns with two glasses and an unlabelled black bottle. There's a marble-topped tea table under the shuttered windows, a big, outmoded Victorian piece that might have come from the hotel parlor. Chiesa drags a second side chair up, sits. He knows I'm not ready to join him.

"The desk clerk would have demanded a place in via Rabata, she tells me," I say.

Chiesa nods. "A good street—she would have done well. But what do you think?"

"This place suits you better. Though Agretta probably didn't think you'd come so cheap."

Through the windows comes a clash of pot lids and a flurry of shouting from the hotel kitchen below. Chiesa pours two glasses of dark liqueur, the mouth of the bottle wavering. "I should have held out for more, you think," he says.

"For your professional ethics? Sure."

"I don't know, *Professoressa*—care of this collection and a place to live? It seemed a good bargain. I'd waited a long time."

"And for that you do what you're told."

"That was the deal, yes."

Street drugs don't deliver this near-appropriate, synthetic calm I'm seeing. Chiesa's using some designer anxiolytic, Valium or one of its derivatives, I think; he's a white-collar addict.

"Who told you what to remove from that box of Inquisitorial records, Signor Chiesa?"

"No one, *Professoressa*," he says. "I honor my agreements— no one needs to stand over my shoulder."

"I want to see those papers."

His tone is sympathetic. "I know you do," he says.

This is what my mother met with when she asked to see things at Palermo's library. This is what she must have felt. In her frustration and her contempt for those clerks she'd resorted to lecturing them like children, but they'd only smiled and waited until she ran down. Chiesa lights a cigarette, drinks with a heavy smoker's casual dexterity, glass and cigarette in the same hand.

"That's complete crap, you know, styling yourself a de Quincey," I say.

He shrugs; the subject doesn't interest him. "Yet here you are," he says.

"I follow up on cross-references, Signor Chiesa. Even the dubious ones."

"The de Quincey didn't send you here."

"No. It referred me to you."

"So? Consult me at the library."

"I won't need to, in fact. I've found a secondary source. The desk clerk's more forthcoming than you."

I can't offend him; he only smiles a little. "Then why are you here, *Professoressa*?" he says.

"To see those papers."

"You think they're here?"

There's a barrister's bookcase on the opposite wall. I go to it and stare hard at the outdated titles behind the glass; I've never liked these kinds of tests.

"I think you're holding each other here, in your imaginary prison," I say.

It's as if I'm all at once alone.

But when I turn around Chiesa stirs himself, stands; he takes too long over the last of his cigarette.

"There's that *girarrosto* in the kitchen, *Professoressa*," he says. "I'll make us up a plate."

He leaves the room with an air of finality. He's going to stay in the kitchen until I find what I've come here for.

It doesn't take long. He hasn't properly hidden it; instead it has its own place in the room, like a second occupant. There's an old farmhouse chair in the corner behind the door, a tall ladderback with heel-gnawed rungs, and there's an accordion folder on its rush seat. It contains a heavy sheaf of old documents, a few written on vellum and bearing the Papal seal, the rest on good paper. I pull out one of the vellum documents. It's clergyman's Latin rendered in a fine bookhand, just like the papers Chiesa felt free to leave in that box of Inquisitorial records. And it's that same determined prelate, that most reverend lord Girolamo Puglisi, again prescribing long, compulsively-detailed abjurations meant to shame even the most insensible rustic.

I take the chair Chiesa meant for me, spread the papers on the tea table. I set the half-drunk bottle and Chiesa's empty glass on the floor, drink my own in two fast swallows and, choking, put it on the floor, too—Chiesa has served up a lethal homemade *amaro*. I shift the papers in front of me, scan them for their sense; I want to find the accused's own words.

I find them in a series of folios whose paper handles like cloth—marvelous stuff—densely written in script. It's the transcript of an interrogation.

Father, I read, *I have not heard about nor know anyone who is a heretic.*

And then the paper is the surface of water, travelled by vague figures; I have to sit back, push it away. In the kitchen Chiesa's begun a long, hacking cough, he's blundering around the room in search of relief. I hear him start the tap, catch water in a glass.

I look through the papers to find the name of the accused. He's identified only as a master—a man of some standing—and his name is Giuseppe Gisira. The words ripple down the page.

Questioned, he replied:

Of witches I do not know if there are any; and of benandanti *I do not know of any others besides myself.*

Questioned further, he replied:

I cannot speak about the others because I do not want to go against divine will.

Questioned, he replied:

I am a benandante *because I go with the others to fight four times a year, that is during the Ember Days, at night; I go invisibly in spirit and the body remains behind; we go forth in the service of Christ, and the witches of the Devil; we fight each other, we with bundles of fennel and they with sorghum stalks. And if we are the victors, that year there is abundance, but if we lose there is famine.*

Questioned: how long have you been involved in this, and are you now? he replied:

It is eight years and more that I have not participated. One enters at the age of twenty and is freed at forty, if he so wishes.

Questioned: how does one enter this company of the benandanti? *he replied:*

Those who have been born with the caul belong to it, and when they reach the age of twenty they are summoned by means of a drum the same as soldiers, and they are obliged to respond.

Questioned: how can it be that we know so many gentlemen who are born with the caul, and nevertheless are not vagabonds? he replied:

I am saying everybody born with the caul must go.

Cautioned to tell the truth about the way one entered in this profession, he replied:

Nothing else happens, except that the spirit leaves the body and goes wandering.

Questioned: who is it that comes to summon you, God, or an angel, a man, or a devil? he replied:

He is a man just like us, who is placed above us all and beats a drum, and calls us.

Questioned: are there many of you who go? he replied:

We are a great multitude, and at times we are five-thousand and more.

Questioned: do you know one another? he replied:

Some who belong to the village know one another, and others do not.

Questioned: who placed that being above you? he replied:

I do not know, but we believe he is sent by God, because we fight for the faith of Christ.

And there's more, pages and pages of interrogations, denunciations, witnesses' depositions soured by ill-feeling or empty of understanding, the inquisitor's conscienceless maneuverings and threats. There are six trials here, six *benandanti* who couldn't keep their secret to themselves. They've been bragging too far afield, confiding in the wrong people. They claim attendance at tumultuous gatherings in the night sky, but their stories don't jibe; some say they've been to games and feasts, others to pitched battles. Their spirits take the form of tiny creatures—mice and birds and crickets—or they are better shadows of themselves, taller, haler, dressed in silk and velvet. Two claim to have cured sick children.

They all fear reprisal from the witches, beatings in bed at night, invisible blows. It's why they must dodge the inquisitor's questions, they say, why at first some of them laugh and pretend to be stupid as sheep. But they've come to discretion too late, and they're no good at it; they're spilling the beans before they know it.

The inquisitor is content to incarcerate these men for months, while their fields go to seed and their wives struggle to undertake the fall slaughter alone. One by one the *benandanti* falter, lose their glibness, or their sincerity, or their circumspection—and flounder desperately after the little hints and admonishments the inquisitor tosses them like picked bones. Witnesses mount against them: their rector, a minor official, an old busybody, one man's wife. The inquisitor neglects for weeks to come from Palermo; he's oiling the machinery of his own appointment to higher office. The *benandanti* languish in their cells, ill, becalmed, remembering sermons of purgatory they thought they hadn't heard. By the end they will say anything, put their mark on anything, if it means they will go home.

And sign they do, in big shaky Xs at the bottom of those long, humiliating abjurations.

Chiesa comes back after a long while, chewing, his face averted. He's torn the chicken to pieces with his fingers and piled it on a plate; he's carrying olives and bread and a dish of green oil. There's a kitchen towel over his shoulder. He gestures at the scattered papers on the table.

"Let's clear this away, eh?" he says. "We'll have a bite to eat."

"You meant these to be found," I say.

He shrugs. "Not everyone would have found them, *Professoressa*."

I study his face, but he's not giving anything away.

"And your deal with the mayor?" I say.

Chiesa sets the plate between us, sits; he wants to eat. "Sometimes researchers find things," he says. "It can't be helped."

"That's true," I say, spitting an olive pit into my palm. "It wasn't any of your doing, was it?"

"Absolutely not. You found them on your own. One can't cry foul over the results of good research skills." He's frowning studiously, pleased with himself.

I can't help it, I have to smile, too—Agretta's going to be furious. "You knew about Piero Quagliata, then," I say. "You knew his probate was there to be found."

His frown fades; his pleasure dims. "No," he says. "I didn't know it was there. That took me entirely by surprise."

I sit back, leave the food to him. He would have removed Piero's probate, had he known it was there—I just found it before he did.

"It's my job to assist researchers, *Professoressa*," he says. "There's nothing that says I must offer what's not asked for."

"But you're hiding material to prevent inquiries."

Chiesa shrugs. "I can't hide it all," he says. "Others will stumble upon things, just as you did."

"So what would you have done if you'd found Piero's probate, Signor Chiesa?" I ask him. "Hidden the entire ledger-book? Or just razored out those pages?"

Chiesa bows his head, puts a hand up to stop me. "I know, I know," he says. "And that's the trouble with this deal, *Professoressa*—it's simply not tenable. I can't do more than I'm doing, not in good conscience. It's already too much. I'm having trouble living with myself." He rubs his forehead hard. "I don't know what I would have done," he says. "Maybe I would have left it where it was."

"Maybe you would have," I say. "For a while."

He lets this pass—he's looking for the bottle of *amaro*. When he finds it he fishes it up off the floor, pours us both a second glass. I don't ask if drinking's such a good idea for him right now. He knows what he's doing. He wipes his fingers in the kitchen towel, lights a cigarette.

"I had a temporary post in Trapani for a while," he tells me, breathing smoke. "One day I look up and there's the librarian, going 'Ssst! Ssst!' and grinning like a bad boy. He wants me to go with him; he's decided that I'm all right, that it's time for my initiation. 'Restricted access!' he whispers, and he takes me back into the storage room behind his office. He shows me a little volume of pornographic doggerel and woodcuts—a very early work and very crude— an extraordinary thing. He kept it locked in a drawer. It wasn't for everyone, he said. I don't know that he was wrong. And every collection has material too fragile to be handled every day, yes? You restrict access—ten handlings a year, whatever makes sense to you—and the eleventh request is turned away. Sympathy but no apology. You know. Restricted access, *Professoressa*—it's common practice. That's what I told myself."

He's going to wish he hadn't said this to me.

I lean back, cross my legs. His eyes follow my calves like he's reading. "You know what, Signor Chiesa?" I say. "I think you're full of shit."

"*Veramente?*" he says. He looks intrigued.

"You're violating fundamental standards of collections care, keeping those papers here," I say. "You know you are. This isn't *restricting access*, for Christ's sake! You're hiding these documents from researchers, and they're not secure—you've

75

destroyed the integrity of the collection. Why don't you just burn them, or throw them in the street? Why not just slice out the pages that aren't convenient? No, Signor Chiesa, you don't toss your professional ethics like this for a crappy apartment, not even for a job like yours. I know you."

He doesn't try to argue with me, or to take back what he's said. He just gets up from the table, hunts around the room in search of an ashtray.

"You thought the *benandanti* ought to be kept quiet, too, didn't you?" I say to his back. "You agreed with the mayor. That's why he got you cheap—a little token bribery, just to put the proper face on things."

"What a thing to say, *Professoressa*," he says. "I don't deserve it." He's still looking for an ashtray.

I just watch him for a moment. It doesn't matter that his nerve—or his conceit—has ultimately failed him, that he's left my initial discovery of the *benandanti* to chance. He's made sure that from that moment of discovery I, or someone like me, could find their way to him, and to the *benandanti's* hidden trials. He's not going to turn me aside now. But he's not going to volunteer anything, either. I wonder about this careful strategy of his, how he's made sure that he can say truthfully to anyone that he's told me nothing.

He finds a plastic ashtray on a swaybacked dropleaf table, carries it back to his chair. He's holding his cigarette like a candle, its long ash upright. If he weren't so thin, I think, this calm of his wouldn't seem like resignation.

I go back through these weeks in Valparuta like a riddle to be solved, a passage to be parsed out for its meaning. There's a secret here, but Sicily's full of secrets; farmers plow up Roman villas and the skulls of *mafiosi* in their fields. Why is this not just one of those?

Chiesa smokes, taking care to keep his eyes from mine.

The answer visits me like a precognition, a jumble of dark forms in water: Chiesa's strangled pride, his wish for me to find him out; the vandalized town, its rancorous people. And *magi* with business cards and telephones, the saints still in residence here like royalty, passing among the people.

My grandmother Origo's dialect comes out of me, archaic, sibilant. "You yourself are of the *benandanti*," I say.

Chiesa doesn't seem to notice. "I've heard of others who claim as much," he says. "But they are not to be believed."

"But you—you have no calling as a *benandante*?"

He chooses muted laughter to put me off. "Oh come, *Professoressa*," he says. "Really now—are you serious?"

I don't answer him. He bursts out laughing then but it's an awful sound, like he's about to vomit his food. I ask him why he's laughing.

"Because these are not matters one should pursue," he says, gasping. "They are against reason." And that retching laughter carries him off again.

I will see later, with regret, that I became Chiesa's inquisitor just then. He put me up to it; he knew he could. There's cant in every line of questioning.

I boxed him in with questions, I made him contradict himself. That tall oppressive room's bad light seemed worse than darkness. I took my lessons from that anxious probate officer—who pulled answers from those *benandanti*'s mouths like hooks from fish—and from the most reverend lord Puglisi himself.

Drunk and medicated, still sobbing with laughter, Chiesa finally says that yes, all right, he's dreamed now and then of fighting witches in dark fields.

And then he lowers his head and blood bursts from his nose and mouth.

CHAPTER EIGHT

Memory is an archive, too, I think, a fossil record.

My father brought me to Rhode Island when I was seven. For the next three years I mistook Providence, with its boarded-up neoclassical facades and ruined neighborhoods, for Palermo's cold double, a city underneath the one I knew and where my mother lived: its shadow, its reflection. I lived with Russell for the academic year in his dark bachelor apartment, spent summers in Palermo with my mother while Russell dug in Busoné, Solunto, Megara Hyblaea. In Russell's living room there were framed posters of museum exhibits, wine magazines on the coffee table; he kept his bedroom door ajar. Women who came up for a nightcap usually stayed.

I fought to stake out territory of my own there, where Russell's solitary interests had claimed every inch for years. It hadn't occurred to him that I could not be added to the décor. I think he hoped to show me sleeping to his more cautious prospects, to push the door of his study open with a finger to his lips and invite the women to peer in with him at me. Not many women could have found their way back into their coats and out the door after that. In Russell's egocentric calculus there had to be profit in good works:

he'd taken me from Sicily, where girls have no chance at life; he'd taken me from my celebrated and increasingly reckless mother.

I remember my father from this time attended by arti- facts: sherds of red- and black-figured vases; jagged necks of lekythoi; bronze wristlets bitten by rust. It seems that they were always with him, though I know this can't be true—I must be thinking of the archaeology lab and Russell working there in the study collection. Yet I see those objects orbiting him like women did, like his students.

I studied them in their felt-lined trays in bad light, all those broken things. The archaeology lab was in an old municipal garage that still smelled of motor oil and paste wax; the hot study lamp added the smell of my father's hair to the room. Everywhere, he seemed too close. I'd gone mute some time before. Whole discourses in Italian had evaporated from my memory, English stood well off yet; I lived for months in an inarticulate rage, with no way to say *A woman once treasured this ruined brooch* or *She kept showing me her fingernails while she talked.*

For years I believed that it was Russell who had broken all the things in those padded trays.

I press the kitchen towel to Chiesa's face and it fills with blood, he puts his head back and pinches his nose shut but blood clogs his throat. He chokes and sprays blood like he's hemorrhaging, more blood than I've ever seen; it's down his chin and shirtfront in a river. There's screaming and sirens in my head, but in fact there's just this busy quiet in the room as we try to get the blood stopped, and that's what finally reminds me that this is not an accident scene, that Chiesa's not a trauma victim. But blood keeps pouring out of him. He drops the sodden towel, pulls his shirttail out and uses that but it soaks through, too; he won't put his head back anymore, won't let me pack his nose. At last he just sits in his chair with his head between his knees and bleeds in a steady stream onto the floor, and I lose my temper—because he's not been hurt, it's just a nosebleed—and it's outrageous for him to sit there like someone's done him in. I shout *Stop it! That's enough, Chiesa!* and he looks up at me in surprise. The bleeding slows. It's stopped by the time he's thought of how to reply.

"I'm sorry, *Professoressa*," he says in a drowned voice. "Please excuse me."

We clean up a little, moving slowly. Chiesa goes into the bathroom, leaning on the furniture, and runs water for a long time. I carry the ruined food into the kitchen and dump it in the trash. Chiesa has only a hotplate and a tiny refrigerator in there, an espresso pot and a single hanging cabinet. A skirt of plaid fabric hides the sink's plumbing. There are no other dishtowels. When I come out of the kitchen he's just leaving the bathroom. He's cleaned the blood from his face and taken off his shirt, and even after all the blood and what I know of his habits, I have to look away from his nakedness. He apologizes again, slips into the bedroom and shuts the door. I feel dizzy and a little sick, like I've lost blood, too.

Later we sit in our chairs again, well away from the bloody table, and finish that deadly bottle of *amaro*. It tastes good now, with that table between us like a slaughtered ox. Chiesa's monosyllabic, stunned; he's developing a blue-black rumor of raccoon eyes, as if his nose has been broken.

This isn't sleight-of-hand he's showing me.

"Chiesa, no one touched you," I tell him.
"That's not for anyone to say," he replies.

We sit for a long time after that, listening to the hotel kitchen's diminishing racket. Chiesa fogs the room with cigarette smoke. At some point, long after the kitchen is quiet and he's begun to talk to me in whispered bursts, he gets up, rummages another bottle from a great ugly linen press, and we drink that one, too. He speaks in flat, rapid sentences, with long silences between; there are still things he's keeping to himself. It's just as well. That awful *digestivo* has nailed me to my chair, slack-limbed, and opened my head like a pomegranate. I sit there in Chiesa's splintered chair and see the things he tells me with hallucinatory clarity, as if I were now de Quincey, dreaming.

All of them, all the *Valparuti*, are either of the *benandanti* or the witches, Chiesa tells me. Those who are not called ally themselves with one faction or the other; no one fails to take sides. For centuries it's been this way. *Forget mayors!* Chiesa hisses. *Forget laws and* polizia *and social classes! Forget trades, professions, occupations, familial duty—forget it all! All those things are subordinate to the night battles here. All that matters is which side you take.*

He talks and talks, carelessly, throwing out his secrets like trash. He was called when he was seventeen, he tells me, and he knew he would be; his mother had been telling him for years that he'd been born a *benandante*. He digs into the neck of the T-shirt he's put on, yanks taut a silver chain there, shows me a locket of good Maltese filigree. It contains the last rusty fragments of the caul he wore at birth. *Twelve Masses were said over it when I was born*, Chiesa says. *It was*

81

baptized with me. My mother gave it to me some months before I was first summoned to the battles, together with the warning that it should always be worn. It protects soldiers from blows. He holds the locket higher, the chain pressing into his jaw. *It causes one's enemy to withdraw.*

He knows that it has failed him. It doesn't seem to matter. He moves on to other subjects, and my imagination blooms in the wake of his voice like phosphorescence.

We go on.

Somehow I find my way back to my rooms, to neutral light and weightless modern furniture. I don't touch anything in there. I lie down on the bed's fragile surface with infinite care, and fall through like a stone into sleep. But the next day we're both back at the library. We stare at each other in disbelief, wondering how the other could be so stupid, why the other didn't think to stay away. Chiesa looks like his face has met a door. I wonder what he's going to tell people—until I remember that everyone is going to think that they already know.

I don't know how to ask him what will happen to him now, how to speak in daylight of the consequences of dreams. All I know is that I was wrong about the mayor and Risacca; they're not *mafiosi*. They believe themselves to be witches, *malandanti*—workers of evil who claim victory when there's famine, who oppose the likes of Chiesa.

What a species of hell their double lives must be. For all of them.

How do they manage it, day to day? How do they do business with each other, believing that four times a year, on a day that can be marked on a calendar, they will work to cut each other to pieces in the dark?

I sit at Chiesa's desk in the archives, transcribing probates, but I'm not seeing furnished rooms or households ready for dispersal. Instead I've got these vivid goblin images that I can't manage, that tell me I'm no stranger to these notions of journeys made in altered states and souls with bodies of their own. I see rivers of armed vermin with human eyes pouring through cold grass, flocks of them rising and falling in the night sky.

I have my grandmother Origo to thank for this.

She could read anything but books—the sky's darkening tint, a faltering wind, the skins of curing cheeses. On Fridays she'd make the beds up early so the spirits could lie down in them, then argue with the fishmonger over a mess of little mullet for the grill. It was all the same to her, the seen and the unseen. The farmhouse in Aidone was where I learned, against my better judgment, to picture the invisible. It rubbed up against the furniture like a cat there, it ran in and out of doors.

And now Chiesa—a peer of mine, a colleague, a man who's been to university—dreams on Ember Thursday nights that he is smoke, sometimes a dun-colored bird. And so do other men in Valparuta, tradesmen and physicians, waiters, lawyers, loungers. They don't agree on details but that doesn't matter much; they all saw the same red, clouded world at birth, when they slid out of their mothers shrouded in the amniotic membrane. That's enough for them. They know that they meet others on those nights, above a distant field somewhere: erstwhile friends, associates, sometimes an uncle they've never liked. They punch each other, pull each other's hair—or they joust, ride the calves and sheep, lay about them with sharp grasses. Those who oppose them have concurring dreams, they know they're witches; it makes no difference that they all seem to misremember where they went and what they did, the shapes of their conscripted souls. They'll know how the battles really went when the harvest is brought in, and then they'll taunt each other, *Yes! Yes! We saw you run away. We were victorious!* And their wives will whisper tales of them lying like the dead those nights, they'll say that they saw voles and little fish wriggle from the caves of their men's open mouths, shinny down the bedclothes and make for the gap under the door.

Let me read this in a monograph somewhere, for God's sake—let me pick it up out of the drifts of paper on my office floor and read it there, in Providence, where there's nothing in the sky but cinders. Here I'm too prone to falling down again, to seeing the weight of spirits on empty beds.

Chapter Nine

The ripples from what Chiesa has done travel outward. I hear the news from the hotel desk clerk two days later.

In the meantime Chiesa has met me daily with careful regard, an irreproachable mix of attention and reserve that I can't deflect without seeming impolite. He brings me *tazzine* of burning-hot espresso from the hotplate in his office; he asks after my comfort and my work, anticipates requests. I know it's calculated but it works anyway, because the dark linen shirts he's chosen to wear are such a terrible mistake. He looks paler than ever in them, the bruises around his eyes even more noticeable. I keep thinking of Piranesi's tiny figure, climbing stairs to nowhere.

I'm not much better myself, dreaming violently at night and waking, waking. I find myself looking into the faces of men on the street for evidence of their calling. I want to know who is with Chiesa, who against him. They mistake me for some crazy trollop, a *sgualdrina*—some stare and follow me, make suggestive remarks. I curse one of them like a guttersnipe to put an end to it, using words and gestures I remember from the Kalsa. He falls away from me, outraged; it's my fault, he shouts, for leading him on.

It's late morning when I encounter the hotel desk clerk.

I should have been at the library an hour ago. Instead I've spent the morning in a kind of limbo, a stranger to myself; I'm not sure what I might do next, what fragment of memory might work its way out like a splinter through my skin to prove that I've a native taste for superstition, that my seeming aversion to it is nothing but hypocrisy. I've let the shower run too long and flooded the bathroom floor; the tiny *scaldabagno* has gone out on me, leaving me to rinse in chilly, iron-tainted water.

I've come to ask the desk clerk why an image of the *Guerrièra* has suddenly appeared on the stairway landing.

I'd noticed it on my way up to my rooms last night: a big, brightly-colored print where a small dim landscape had hung before. I'd imagined the hotel manager on a stepstool in midday, tack hammer in hand, changing pictures on a whim—while the housekeeping staff backed up behind him on the stairs, unable to get by.

It's a piece worthy of some disruption, this portrait of the Warrior-Girl.

She's a hero from Sicilian fables, one of the tall, elegantly-articulated *marionette* who fight and love and trick each other, again and again, on the rickety stages of Sicily's puppet theaters. In this portrait the *Guerrièra* stands right up against the picture's frame, uncomfortably close to the viewer; it's just what she would do.

The effect is astonishing. She stands there wooden, smiling, aggressive, her steeply-keeled breastplate shining like brushed steel. Her handsome face is round as a girl's but strangely implacable; a fantastically-bladed lance juts up beside her—she is holding it, I know, in a slim mailed fist just below the picture's frame. The *Guerrièra* is blonde and blue-eyed, exotic traits on this island; her pale hair falls straight and unnaturally smooth from beneath her visored helmet to

her shoulders, where it curls under just a bit in the sort of
crop affected by medieval noblemen. Behind her stretches
an indefinite landscape: rows of dark, flame-shaped cedars;
a brook whose flow seems to defy gravity; a cluster of distorted spires in an opaque distance. The *Guerrièra* is lively,
deadly, fine and brutal—and suspiciously friendly, it seems to
me, like a sphinx. I'd looked at her a long time, half in love.

In the hotel lobby the restaurant is closed, though I can
smell the lunch menu's preliminaries: sautéed onions and a
pot of fava beans simmering in the kitchen. A single guest
is checking out, a downcast fellow in a suit of tiny checks
that makes him look like he has dressed in newsprint. He's a
salesman, I think, someone from out of town whose visit has
gone badly. The desk clerk is whittling him down further;
he doesn't know what to do with her beauty or her silence.
He wants to talk to her, tell her his troubles. She accommo-
dates him like an empty room.

No one from the mayor's office even called on me, the
man says forlornly. What am I to do with such indifference?

I visit those stolen gravegoods in their cabinet while she
finishes him off. They're worn like river rocks, beautifully
patinaed; the figured vase shows sprinting men with barrel
thighs and sprightly, pointed penises. They chop the air with
the heels of their hands. Nothing is labelled—the objects
have been left to speak for themselves. I wonder if anyone
still remembers where they came from.

The desk clerk tells me that the print I think has just
appeared has been there all along.

That can't be true, I say. I would have noticed it.

She shrugs; I deserve no more indulgence than the man
in the checked suit. "Perhaps it's your notice that has only
just arrived," she says, "and not the picture." She busies her
hands on the counter between us, gathering the man's hotel

bill, but her eyes hold mine. "The Elimo is a good hotel, *Professoressa*—it's not like your home," she says. "Perhaps you should pay us more attention."

I understand that this is both rebuke and invitation, but to what I'm not yet sure.

She flicks the man's hotel bill with her fingers. "This one, he's just like you," she says. "He comes here for a meeting, nothing else—he won't avail himself of our services. He doesn't browse our art, dine in our restaurant, read the paper in our parlor—nothing. He's waiting for his meeting! And then—*pouf!*—there is no meeting. It's cancelled by the mayor's office. So he goes home with nothing for his money, when we have been here all along, ready to offer him a little pleasure, a little something out of the ordinary to take home with him. It's not wise, *Professoressa*, fixing one's sights so narrowly like that. You lay yourself open for disappointment. I've seen it many times."

"He was to meet with the mayor's people?"

"With the mayor himself, I think," the desk clerk says indifferently. "He is the cousin of the mayor's sister-in-law, and came looking for a post."

"Agretta turned him away, then."

She gives me a look of gentle scorn. "Of course not, *Professoressa*," she says. "His office sent sincere regrets—the mayor was indisposed."

"Indisposed?"

"He's been taken ill, it seems. I'm told that he is not improving."

Sirens go off in my head again, the dopplering wail of speeding rescue units, fire trucks. The ormolu clock in the parlor behind me chimes into the silence.

"When did this—?"

"Several days ago." The desk clerk never flinches, never takes her eyes from mine. "He and Signor Chiesa were struck down the same night."

She watches me a moment longer, to make sure that I have understood her. Then she turns back to the mailboxes behind her, to the hotel keys on their brass hooks, the phone and fax and vertical files. She's forgotten the hotel bill in her hand.

"You see?" she calls back to me. A ragged edge has crept into her voice. "You should avail yourself of our services, *Professoressa*—ask us just in passing what we might have for you. We're here to assist our guests, you know. In any way we can. You do us an honor when you call upon our hospitality."

I watch her as she moves behind the counter, papers shivering in her hand. She's an ally of Chiesa's, one in sympathy with the *benandanti*.

"I've been remiss, not noticing your *Guerrièra*," I say.

The desk clerk keeps her back to me; we have an understanding. "She is very fine, is she not?" she says.

Chapter Ten

The bomb that killed Simona Origo and the Palermitan prosecutor she was riding with had been planted in a sewer drain on via Malaspina and detonated remotely, probably from the balcony of a high-rise apartment nearby. I read that the force of the blast drove one of the armored car's seat springs into my mother's vagina. It also tore the prosecutor's right arm off at the shoulder and left his belt buckle embedded in his chest. I was seventeen when it happened. I hadn't seen or heard from my mother in seven years.

For a few days the traffic in and out of Russell's apartment changed. Colleagues came to grip his shoulder and murmur guarded sympathies; the women stayed away, sent pastel cards in the mail. Old rivals telephoned, and I listened to my father's half of each exchange, veiled boasts and gropings after the expected sentiments. I don't know what he really felt. I heard him say again and again that had she known she was to die this way she would have accepted it like flattery, an end like this that threw her straight into legend. She would have appeared to push it away while thinking it her due. But even that was cant; Russell didn't know.

Because what Palermo understood of car bombings—what they did to flesh and bone, their final assemblages of wreckage and limbs—had come from Simona Origo. She'd gone to those scenes for everyone else, framed them into compositions that were nearly bearable, that could be taken in. Her photographs omitted the awful smell of things not meant to burn, the scrape and dry voices of investigation, the wider perspective of road, buildings, landscape and sky left untouched. But she had known all those things. No, she would have refused such a deadly, empty compliment. She would have turned it aside, shuddering.

"Well, she's done it, hasn't she?" my father said to me at the end of that strange week. "Now she's part of the fucking cause." He'd been carrying a bottle of bourbon around the apartment all night, working on it.

I'd thrown sheets over all the lamps, pained by their illumination; it seemed to me that everything should have changed, gone black at its edges. And now I wondered how such a big man as my father could appear so small.

He'd been convinced for years, I think, that he would be what caused the death of her.

I consider leaving Valparuta. Chiesa's anxious attentions are what remind me that I could—and that anyone else probably would, irreparably spooked by what they'd seen. But for me it's not that simple.

Where else would I go?

I almost say this to Chiesa one afternoon, while he's apologizing for the crushing heat. July is hard upon us; the days smoke like hot ashes, white and pungent with dust. I almost say *Where else would I go?* to him, admit that I've run hard aground here, because I've thought about that transient's room off the beach in Mondello and all the barren *pensioni* I could stay at, one after another, to no purpose.

Instead I tell him that I tolerate heat well, that it's the motion of the sea I can't abide. This isn't true—I don't get seasick. But it's the closest I can come to telling him the truth.

He's stopped us in the library vestibule again, a favorite place of his. He likes these kinds of no man's lands. We've come from the *caffè* bar across the piazza, where we've each had an *espresso doppio* in an effort to revive ourselves. The vestibule is like an oven, filled with the afternoon's hard slanting light.

"I wondered if you might be contemplating a short *vacanza, Professoressa*," Chiesa says carefully. He doesn't want to give me any ideas. "A few days away from here, perhaps, where it's cooler? Evidently not to the beach, though, if the sea distresses you."

I look him in the face so that he knows I'm onto him. "Do you think that I'm afraid of you?" I say.

He laughs a little, looks at the floor. "No," he says. "That's the last thing I'd expect you to be."

"What, then?"

He'd wanted to avoid this. "Impatient with us, perhaps," he says unhappily. "Unsympathetic."

I study him in the unforgiving light. He's forgotten how bad he looks, bruised and cachectic in his stylish suit, like a man who's run afoul of his creditors. I'm only demeaning him further, letting him think that he must ingratiate himself to keep me here. I wish he'd guess that I'd done myself in back in Providence, and that I have no option but to stay. I like him best when he's high-handed as a prince.

"I'm an anthropologist, Signor Chiesa," I say. "I have work to do. I've no time for vacations."

"You'll stay on, then," he says.

"I will, yes," I tell him. "But if you bring me one more cup of that wretched coffee of yours, I'm leaving."

He stares at me, affronted, then bursts into harsh laughter.

CHAPTER ELEVEN

Chiesa has diazepam to help him through these long, premonitory days; I have my work. The two are not so very different. It's what I've resorted to for years now. I go on compiling my lists of lost possessions, throwing them up around me like bulwarks: heaps of furniture, crockery, metalware, glass and silver; clothing, shoes, hats and jewelry; paintings, tapestries, votives; tools, carts, carriages and barrows; bushels of wheat and crops left to fall in the fields. They're all gone now, all these things—their particles have dispersed into dust and earth, into smoke chambered up in clouds. I amass nothing but their irretrievability in recalling them like this. Nothing is restored.

Did I imagine that my lists would somehow conjure up these lost things? Did I think there was a saturation point that I could reach, a moment at which everything destroyed would, all at once, precipitate out, fall from the sky, rise from the ground?

Did I?

I'm beginning to suspect that they are nothing but memorials, my lists.

I miss Vergone, I discover—his determined historylessness, his hard joky edge. I miss our random couplings.

We'd go occasionally to his place on Angell Street, always in the middle of the day; we'd decide on it the way you might decide to go and grab a sandwich. Vergone owned a fifth of a condoed-out Victorian mansion a few blocks from campus, a hollow, elegant place that echoed like a warehouse. We never bothered with much ceremony there. We'd end up on the couch, the floor, slammed up against the door; Vergone would put his weight on one arm and open his belt one-handed, grinning. Sometimes I'd push him off and put my weight on him, take the short hairs at his nape in my fist until his grin faded.

Afterwards we'd lie breathing where we'd fallen, not touching, and feel something close to tolerance for each other.

I'd say his name, *Vergone*, and make a joke of it; *vergogna*, I'd say, for shame.

It's the heat, I tell myself, that brings this false nostalgia on. I'm sleeping at night in knotted sheets, provoked by my own warmth. If I could I'd order my own body, like a tiresome lover, from my bed, and let my thoughts sleep alone.

They need the solitude. Chiesa has begun to remind me of Vergone, for God's sake, a mad association; all they share between them is a faint echo of a type—the same dark coloring, perhaps, and a build inclined toward spareness. They are nothing alike, those two. I wonder what kind of trick I'm playing on myself, letting one lead to the other.

Chiesa, in the meantime, has troubles of his own. The mayor's illness has left him without an advocate in the *municipio*; money for library operations has evaporated. He can't get his funds for acquisitions, can't even get the city to approve a requisition for supplies. He buys toilet tissue and file folders with his own money, though his last paycheck has been mysteriously delayed. His days at the library become a protracted *passeggiata*, a promenade before his neighbors—the jealous ones, the ill-wishers, the merely curious, his anxious backers. They all watch him with hooded eyes, judging his condition. Chiesa's self-consciousness is acute. He abandons all but the most ceremonial of behaviors—the civil servant's lukewarm handshakes, languid scribbling and petty obstructionism—and says nothing that isn't platitude or commonplace.

But when he comes into the archives he stands beside me in my chair, stands there with his palms on my desk, watching the empty aisles of the stacks as if there were people there whispering or a complex tableau taking place in mid-air. It's the drugs he's on, detaching and elaborating his paranoia so that he can watch it pass before him like a procession.

"Signora Corrao refuses to pay her late fees," he tells me. "She is waiting for the new librarian."

They do this, the Sicilians—they've known for years that their venal, incompetent bureaucrats can only favor or forget them when swept in or out of office.

I look up at Chiesa but his face is calm; only his eyes move, their color eclipsed. "She could be backing the wrong horse," I say. "You might keep your post."

"If Agretta recovers, maybe—but I doubt it."

"If he recovers? If?"

Chiesa pays no attention. "No, he'll fire me if he does. I've screwed him all along."

"Maybe he'll figure it was me, Chiesa—sticking my nose in where it didn't belong, pressing you for answers you didn't want to give. Maybe he'll excuse you."

"No, the whole enterprise is in flames now, and I'm to blame—it was I who convinced him that it couldn't fail."

He hangs his head, sheepish; the memory still pleases him. "What did I care what lies I told? I would have said anything, anything—I was dreaming of these books in their musty tomato cartons, I saw water covering the floor, mice. A disaster was imminent, I thought, I was seeing it. So I told him: we could stand on each other's backs for this, just this once. We could set aside our differences." Chiesa looks away, discomfited. "Agretta wore his ambition like a blindfold over his eyes," he says. "It should not have been so easy."

"Your success has overtaken you, you think."

"Maybe. A rustic would have known that the wheel always turns."

"A rustic wouldn't have been dreaming of books in boxes."

"Oh, yes," he says. "There's progress for you, eh?"

He leaves me then, irritated, his leather heels brisk and quiet on the marble floors.

The page before me is useless, chewed to lace by insects. I tap the book's spine on the desk, salt its surface with tiny, burst carapaces the color of sloughed skin.

But then he comes to my rooms that night in the day's crumpled trousers and undershirt, beltless, in stockinged feet. He knocks at my door once, then again, then again, each time more softly, to persuade me to give up all pretense of absence or sleep and let him in. He knows I'm here, staring in the dark. But when I crack the door and look out at him in the overlit hallway he steps back and lets his arms fall, showing me his full hands, his helplessness. Like an evacuee he seems to have snatched whatever came to hand in his rush out the door, his cigarettes, a small glass, two blood oranges, an unopened bag of *biscotti*.

"I've nothing to drink, *Professoressa*," he says.

He has a small, neat arc of broken skin on his forearm—a bite mark. "That's all right," I say. "You've brought everything else."

I push the door open, let the hall's slanting, unkind light cut shadows under the wine bottle on my sitting-room table, the half-empty glass and torn cellophane wrappers there. I've been eating crackers stolen from the hotel restaurant. There's a book on its face on the floor, a stir of papers, shoes under the table, clothing on the chairback.

"You've been bitten," I say, and switch on the lamp.

"You've been sitting in the dark, drinking."

"You would have been, too, I'll bet, had you thought to stop at the bar on your way up to your rooms."

"He gave you a bottle? The bartender?"

"I made it look like I meant to sit in his bar unescorted and drink."

Chiesa shakes his head; the oranges roll dangerously on the unsteady table. "What a Turk you are, *Professoressa*," he says. "We have no hope of reaching you."

I hear my grandmother again in his words, the world divided into Turks and Christians. I tell myself that I will never get used to hearing Sicily's archaic vernacular from the archivist.

"I have some peroxide for that. Sit down," I tell him, and go rummage the tiny medicine cabinet in my bathroom. A black millipede has come up the drain to lie in the sink. When I come back to the sitting room Chiesa is peeling an orange, parting it into sections. He stops this delicate work to swab at his arm with a kind of polite thoroughness; he has no faith in this wound-cleaning business.

"I don't have any holy water," I say.

He's careful not to look at me. "And why should you?" he says. "You travel with antiseptic."

"I don't suppose you saw what bit you."

"No."

"You were upstairs?"

He cups the stained cotton ball and pieces of orange rind in his palm, carries them to the wastebasket. "I was reading. They find their way in, you know—insects, vermin. These old edifices are breeding grounds for such things."

I nod as if I understand. "There's one of those Horribles in my sink," I say.

"There, you see? Leave it to me, *Professoressa*—I'll rid you of it."

I hear the eggshell crackle of the millipede's exoskeleton as Chiesa crushes it against the porcelain. He's wiping the bowl clean when I come up behind him in the bathroom. I rest my hands on his sides, let my lips brush the wing of his shoulder blade. In the mirror I see his face give, go soft as a child's and then crimp with pained confusion.

"Lift up your shirt for me, won't you?" I say.

He turns awkwardly, dropping his shoulder into the tight space between us to ease me away from him. It's what one does on a crowded bus for a little breathing room, nothing personal, just a mild assertion of will.

I give him his space, lean in the open doorway, holding my elbows. "They're still tormenting you, aren't they? Your enemies." *Those bold witches*, I want to hiss. *I malandanti spavaldi.*

Without a word he pulls his shirt out of his trousers, tents it up over his thumbs. But the most distressing thing isn't the faint sooty streaks of bruising or the tiny cuts like dolls' red smiles along his ribs; it's his scaphoid, shrunken belly, the loose skin over his navel lying in thin folds like draped silk.

I should not have tried to use him so carelessly; Chiesa never agreed to it.

"Forgive me," I say.

He yanks his shirttail down. "I wouldn't show you, you thought, but perhaps you could get me to undress?"

"I didn't want to ask you."

"It was easier to seduce me."

"Not easier, no. I—"

"Risacca was right," he says. "There is something wrong with you."

I've forgotten what it's like to wound unintentionally, I've chosen my targets with so little discrimination for so long. And I've forgotten how to apologize. I scrub a hand over my mouth like I'm clearing dirt from a stone. "Look, Chiesa," I say. "What's happening here should be interesting behavior to me, nothing more. It should be cultural phenomena, folk tradition—"

"You make me tired," he says. "I've read those books, too."

He pushes past me, back into the dark sitting room where the air smells of orange peel and damp paper, the day's trash. He has the right to take what he needs from me now, and it's not sex or some diversion of his thoughts but a place to wait out the terrors infesting his rooms. He moves around the table, sets the glass he's brought with him upright and pours us both overfull, then carries his glass to the armchair. I've offended him; he won't sit with me. He twitches one trouser leg up as he sits.

But there are colored tailings of drugs in his blood and he's half starved; the darkness and wine work on him quickly, breaking him down into his simpler parts. Before long he's talking. He takes pains to keep me with him, prompting me for questions. He's a circumspect ecstatic, unwilling to be left alone with his visions—or he's using me, a proven weapon, to bring truth out of him.

I sit and eat the blood orange Chiesa has peeled, its small rubbery wedges bursting in my mouth. The fruit tastes like boxed wine and Orangina, grocery store flavors, neither bloody nor mysterious. A large pale moth slaps the ceiling like a disembodied hand.

"In Padua, at library school, there was an archive I would visit in my sleep," Chiesa says. He turns his glass against the inadequate light, sips the black liquid. "An immense place, its walls in darkness. The stacks rose up into a vault and disappeared in haze."

It's easy to see him there, thin and pensive, his smeared image reflected in a vast grey floor. He wouldn't stand there long—he'd strike off into the towers of books like a creature adapted to cities.

"What do you think my work was there?" His gaze falters; he fears that it might seem a dubious post. "I'd press the sound of a barking dog into a file folder, perhaps with the calves of a woman I'd seen climbing on the bus. My mother's hands and the smell of my father's breath I boxed in paper the color of earth, reams of it. My fiancée's tongue like a velvet ribbon—into a locked case. You see?"

"Your subconscious, ordered into series and subseries."

"My efforts to do so."

I want to ask him: *A fiancée?* I take hold of the bag of *biscotti*, experimentally, but it crackles like a twig fire. I leave both alone.

"Everyone conducts night work," I say.

"But the *capo* found me there," Chiesa says.

"What?"

"Every season at the Ember Days." He's squinting, still trying to make out how this could have been. "I'd lost track of Saints' Days, my Naming Day, rogations, *feste*, everything—it didn't matter. He found me with his drum. I had a document in my hands one night, dreaming—something on red vellum, a long list of protestations. I'd been in Padua barely three weeks and I hated myself, I felt medieval, chinked, windowless, I thought I smelled of cooking fires. Already I'd been reading the cultural studies—Monter, Ginzburg, Midelfort—those excellent historical treatises on the *benandanti*. Our merit lay in our remoteness, our historicity, like cavemen, do you see? And there I was—! I wore my calling like a stinking pelt. But still the *capo* came with his drum, pounded me out of that nighttime archive and carried me off to fight. And then again. And again. For two years. In classes the next day I understood nothing, I thought black crickets swarmed the stairwell of the lecture hall."

"It's in you like a stain, you're telling me." Why did I think I wouldn't hear this from the archivist?

He gets up, staggering a little, upends the bottle over his glass. "No," he says. "I'm telling you that for us, it's all the same. We are so easily swayed."

Swayed, yes—but never moved. Like carcasses suspended from hooks, laundry from balconies. I remember my mother's followers, the agitation of limbs and voices necessary to stay mired in the old ways.

"Something's gotten to Agretta, too," I say.

"Up through the plumbing, perhaps," Chiesa says, but it's a low joke.

"Have his colleagues turned on him? Do they beat him in his bed?"

Chiesa has fallen back down into the armchair. He holds his glass at eye level, pretends to consult its meager depths. "No, *Professoressa*," he says. "He has fallen ill."

There's a strangely unsettled evening during this time, an ocher-colored dusk accompanied by a buffeting, direction-less wind that comes up out of season. It's a Friday; I can't help thinking of spirits out looking for repose in the bed-rooms of the living. I return early to the Elimo to take pos-session of my freshly made-up bed, turning down the covers while it's still light to forestall presumptuous spirits. I don't ask myself what it is I'm doing.

I've bought a *girarrosto* chicken of my own this time, avoiding the desk clerk's pointed gaze as I carry it, reeking, across the lobby. On the stairs the *Guerrièra* seems to wear the desk clerk's same expression on her own smooth face.

I've come in too early. The evening ravels out over a stretch of hours, punctuated by the slam and bated vacuum of the wind. Someone has opened a window to air my rooms; the long opaque drapes ripple against the darkened glass like vertical sheets of water. I try to read but find myself listening instead, waiting for the weather to declare itself in a rumble of thunder or a scatter of rain against the windows. But a storm won't put me any more at ease. It never rains in Sicily in mid-July—never.

Chiesa doesn't come. He's shown up twice since that first evening, each time with the same marks of haste on him, carrying keys and food and maybe a wadded handker-chief, once with a red ear and a handprint on his face. For an hour he'd shouted over the ringing in his injured ear, unable to hear my questions.

There's no difference between these invisible blows and the torment Chiesa endures now at the hands of the City Council. Both are occult, proportionless; neither can be accounted for. He's called to chambers, left waiting, sent away, called back, chided, given a nest of old forms to complete. Some sort of inquiry has been set in motion—never mind that every one of those hypocrites took money or favors from Agretta to approve the archivist's hire. They're trying to drive him out, Chiesa tells me. But it's all bloodletting from small cuts, I think, the work of torturers. To simply fire Chiesa would cost them nothing.

There will be no other posts for him.

I've been watching him there at the library as he belittles his patrons, wearing the remains of his black eyes like an expensive accessory. With him so reduced I think I can see it, his ribs sprung and curved to hold books and manuscripts, not this hardened heart he's showing everyone. Chiesa carries Valparuta's archives within himself, he was built to house them; he has no other purpose.

If my bones had purpose mapped on them like that I might stand where I was, too, and let them gut me, set me ablaze.

Outside, the wind saws against the building like a train taking a curve. I look up, startled at the noise; the open window is breathing like a mouth, the drapes lifting and shivering all the way up their length. I cross the room, push my hands between the curtains and shut the window with a bang.

The smell of picked bones in my wastebasket colors my sleep. I dream of greasy, interrupted feasts, quantities of food left for me to graze at my leisure.

CHAPTER TWELVE

It's the desk clerk with her brand of shrouded, hard assistance who tells me, the next day, what came in on that strange wind. She seems the only one in Valparuta who's at ease with all she knows, who carries the invisible into the waking world the same way one carries a sextant on a voyage, to stay a course. Afterward, when I go out into the ruins of the day, I'm sure that wind felt dense to me, too, and dangerous, like surf inhabited by sharks.

It seems a morning like any other—steepening sun, birds singing under the eaves—but I find the hotel lobby strangely deserted and smelling strongly of decay, as if the room's weary *fin de siècle* opulence has somehow gone off in the heat. There's no one behind the desk. I don't think much of this, since every establishment has its good days and its bad, but when I open the door to the street I know that something larger is amiss.

It's the whole town that's taken on the smell of a burst trash bag, not just the Elimo's lobby; some peculiar domestic carnage has taken place during the night. Wine and milk and oil have been poured out in the gutters in long slicks of red and green and bluish-white. Far down the street I see a man in shirtsleeves crouching on the pavement, a ceramic pitcher upended in his hand. It seems that half of Valparuta's kitchens have dumped their liquids in the street. A small wooden cask lies in the gutter outside the hotel door, bleeding wine.

There's been no rain during the night, no storm.

The desk clerk is standing on the hotel steps smoking a cigarette. When she hears me she turns without haste and her expression doesn't change; I'm just one more item that needs managing today. She already knows what she will do with me.

"Good morning, *Professoressa*," she says. She's conscious of the irony in her greeting but will not stoop to it.

She smokes with studied grace, one arm wrapped across her body and her cigarette held negligently in curled fingers. She's like a deep lake, the Elimo's desk clerk—nothing disturbs her for long.

I ask her what it is I'm seeing here, what's happened in the night to cause such wholesale ruin.

She tips her head toward the rancid slurry in the street. "It's all gone bad, *Professoressa*," she says. "It wasn't fit to feed a cat."

"All this went bad overnight?"

"The *orda furiosa* got to it," she says. "We're not as careful as we ought to be."

I have a sudden vision of the air here thick with spirits, passing overhead like schools of fish and hunting, always hunting. This furious horde wasn't Friday's usual migration of weary, benign spirits, out looking for a bed.

"You knew they were coming," I say.

She exhales smoke through pursed lips, a sigh of disgust. "Yes, *Professoressa*, it's no secret when they come," she says.

"But some people, you know, can have a timetable in their hands and still miss a train. I don't pretend to understand it. That cask you see there, lying in the street? The hotel barman left the bung out overnight—and his sister is one who attends the furious horde! He of all people should have remembered to seal his bottles and kegs. It's sheer brainlessness to me, *Professoressa*—or perhaps we have a fondness for misfortune."

But a guywire has snapped somewhere, the one that holds the moment up like curtains; the whole thing comes down around me in a giant wave of déjà vu. That little keg, its rotund form lying in a dark pool of its own making, the attendant flies—it looks like one of Simona Origo's crime scene photographs.

"Who could mistake that wind?" the desk clerk says. "That should have made anyone stop and wonder, don't you think?"

"I don't know." I reach for the cigarette in her fingers; I'm going to vomit if I don't fill my nose and lungs with something other than this smell of spoilage. "I thought a storm was coming."

The desk clerk thinks I must be joking; no one could be as ignorant as this. "At this time of year?" she says. "Surely not, *Professoressa!*"

She has passed me her smoke without hesitation, turning it upright between her fingers as if I were her closest *amica*. But she watches me take my quick little nonsmoker's hits off it with a critic's unbending eye. When I hand the cigarette back to her, she tosses it into the wet gutter as if it has turned to trash in my mouth.

"Come inside with me, *Professoressa*," she says. "I have some information at the desk for you."

What she tells me there gains force from being offered,
like advice to travellers, over the hotel's mahogany desk. I
put my foot on the brass toe rail and lean in to listen; the
desk clerk sets a colored tourist's map of Valparuta on the
counter between us, as if she's going to show me how to find
the *chiesa matrice* or the Norman *rocca*. The map is a diplopic
four-color print job, magenta halos around its words and
universal icons; I wonder whose hallucinatory optimism has
produced it.

But the desk clerk knows what it's good for. She marks
a handful of small Xs all around the city's twisted, enclosed
streets, taps her pen on one.

"Until last August, Signor Spadafora's bookbindery
was here," she tells me. "The Signore went to Trapani for a
hernia repair and something went wrong—his belly filled
with blood and they couldn't save him. Anna Asaro, whose
house is here—" she shifts her pen—"fell down dead among
her chickens this past winter, only thirty-six years old.
Augusto Minniti was killed in a car crash two years ago.
The housepainter Ruzzolone fell from a scaffold, and little
Laura Fuga—her family lives here—died of an infection of
the brain."

"Their lives were all cut short," I say.

"Yes." The desk clerk traces a circuitous route across
the city with the pen's tip. "The hotel barman's sister says
that she has lately seen them all, *Professoressa*—dreadfully
transformed—among the furious horde."

I look away, wishing that I disbelieved her, but there's
nothing here that says that what she's told me isn't possible.
The lights are off in the lobby this morning, and in the
dimness the room's oversized wing chairs and heavy console
tables lie couched around like animals. You wait for them to
stir, to heave up to their feet.

"It came as no surprise, of course, her seeing them like that," the desk clerk says. "All those snatched away from life must follow *Donna* Perchta."

"That isn't a Sicilian name."

The desk clerk draws a sketchy crossbow in the map's margin, loads it with a V-tipped arrow. "No," she says. "No one knows who *Donna* Perchta is, *Professoressa*—no one has ever seen her face. She leads, and so always goes before. She never turns back." The desk clerk is attempting what might be a headdress or an elaborate coiffure; she scribbles it out.

"*Donna* Perchta dresses for the hunt," I say.

"That's what the others tell us, yes. I think it must be so."

I watch her pen strike lines through her drawings—*no, no, no.* "Those who are snatched away from life—they follow Perchta like her hounds," I say.

She seems as unhappy as I am with this thought. "Well, they can hardly help it, *Professoressa*," she says. "Their spirits are debased by their misfortune; they join Perchta still burdened with their sins. It changes them, you know. They require prayers and masses to restore them to God's arms."

I hunch my shoulders like a truculent hotel guest, put all my weight on the counter. "Who tells you these things?" I say. "The barman's sister? The one who for a fee will carry a message to your dead uncle who—what, fell under a train?"

The desk clerk looks at me with faint amusement; I'm making an ass of myself. "Not messages, *Professoressa*," she says. "You may as well try sending letters to a wolf! No, we send them little gifts to console them, small dark things. They don't recognize us anymore."

She pushes the souvenir map towards me then, marked with her attempts to guide me to another place. "No one needs to tell us this, *Professoressa*," she says. "We've known it all along. You'd do well to value our experience—we only wish to make your stay more pleasant. *Prego*," she says, "take this with our compliments."

I fold the map in half, run my thumbnail down the crease. Neither of us knows whether this means I'm going to keep the map or throw it away.

Discarding it will do no good. I'm stuck now with this blunt cognizance she's lent me, and I am so volatile now that it's as if I've stood in the path of the furious horde and seen them myself: all those dead before their time, robbed of memory, rushing like a great wind over the earth, ruining everything in their path. Victims of accidents, strokes, drownings, killings; children dead of cholera, whooping cough, weak hearts, falls. They are feral, deformed, drawn on by the faceless *Donna* Perchta, and they carry with them the weight of their unabsolved sins: the greedy weighed down by bags of useless money; the dishonest shouldering their most flagrant lies, bushels of bad grapes sold too dear, naked, squirming mistresses grown big as statues and heavy as brass. And the children, poor things, hobbled by original sin, none of their own doing.

Simona Origo would have been among them for a time. Carrying her self-absorption, maybe—an enormous lead-framed mirror, held before her face.

I wish there were someone I could hit for giving me such thoughts, a body I could walk over like a bridge, away from these laughable, appalling notions. But the desk clerk is impervious to blows, I'm sure of it—and I could no more strike her than I could smash that lovely plundered, figured vase in the case behind me.

She leaves me then, the desk clerk, as if she knows she's hamstrung me. She doesn't excuse herself, doesn't wish me a good day. But she has a gliding, nearly motionless walk that masks her peremptoriness, makes it less than cruel: instead of

walking away from me she appears to have been carried off
on a slow current.

Outside, pedestrians skirt the wine cask's still form. Ants
and a few vicious-looking hornets have joined the flies at the
edge of the thickening pool beneath it. It looks like sudden
death, like passersby avoiding a body in the gutter.

A book of Simona Origo's photographs was published after
she died, a brittle-spined folio volume with stiff, glossy
pages that smelled of their resin coating. Russell picked one
up somewhere; he probably has it still. I never looked at
it. I didn't need to—I'd seen all those photographs before,
in my mother's apartment. She'd had her studio there, or
rather she'd simply lived in the midst of her work. Black
and white prints were scattered about in every room, curled
like leaves.

This is what I learned from those photographs:

A man shot in a cul-de-sac looks like a plank laid out
across the pavement. A young upstart killed in a sedan's back
seat looks like he's sleeping—except for the blood mapping
his face and the awful spattered interior of the car. Dry saplings, crates, parked cars and corrugated awnings all look like
they were brought in later to explicate the scene; everything
around an ugly death, I've learned, speaks like art.

There were other subjects, too—grainy, tilted images
of moments on the street, candid shots of naked children,
moribund old counts and countesses at cocktail parties—
but the crime scene photographs were what made Simona
Origo's reputation. My mother had no technique but her
instinct; her best photos were of the dead and objects in
trajectory, birds in flight, a shifting crowd, things she could

not influence. Her posed shots inevitably suffered from her intervention. Her judgment was poor, her hand too heavy.

For decades now I have not pictured her. That bomb dismembered her entirely, in fact and in my mind. Afterward there didn't seem to be enough left whole to make a proper memory.

I work for days to forget the image of Simona Origo among the ranks of the furious horde.

Chapter Thirteen

A rumor starts around: Mayor Agretta will attend a reception at the home of *Cavalière* Grado, his old friend and supporter. He's going to leave his sickbed to honor the invitation.

I hear the idle men in front of the tobacconist's debating what this means in heated whispers. *Il Cavalière*, they say, has grown impatient with the mayor, he wants to see some effort. What's the point of buying influence, after all, if your man won't get out of bed for you?—*But then*, they mutter, taken aback by their own callousness, *a man crushed by sorcery deserves some consideration, too.* They don't know where to put their sympathies. In their confusion of feeling they seem the gentlest of people.

But their scruples won't prevent them all from standing in the street outside the *Palazzo* Grado to see Agretta's condition for themselves. Like weathermen they discuss the predictive value of the symptoms they might see: pallor, wasting, weeping sores, ague. They want to know if the mayor's doomed, if he's resisting his demise. In fact they are like vultures in their tweed *coppole*, interested in the kind of feast misfortune brings.

They're the ones I'm going to follow. I have to see for myself, too—not whether the mayor is likely to survive or not, but whether this illness of his speaks to me of an invisible hand.

I ask Chiesa if he wants to go. It's expected that the mayor will speak, I tell him; I've heard that the *Palazzo* Grado's front façade has a twisting double staircase of white marble that mounts to the *piano nobile*, an elevation the mayor, with his weakness for oratory, has found irresistible in the past.

Chiesa looks up at me with reddened eyes. He's hunched over an old teacher's desk in the library's back room, the place where he smokes and makes his molten *caffè* and more and more often, I think, sleeps. There's a chrome waiting-room couch with thin orange cushions against one wall that seems just vacated, marked with the impression of a shoulder and hip. It looks like it could still be warm.

Chiesa sighs. I think he wishes I were not so ill-bred. "*Professoressa*," he says, "there'll be nothing to see. Just a sick man anxious for his reputation, attempting to overcome his malady."

I sit down on the dented couch. Its cushions are cool, not warm at all. "No, Chiesa, we'd go to hear him speak," I say.

"He won't say anything."

"But he must speak. It's a public appearance, he's trying to shore up support—"

Chiesa's chair shrieks as he swivels to face me. "Of course he'll speak, *Professoressa*—if his strength permits it. But he won't say anything. You'll be left to think what you like."

I get up to prowl the narrow room, fake an interest in the curling notices taped to the wall. There's a single small, grated window set deep in the wall near the ceiling. Chiesa chooses at every turn to occupy a prison.

"Some are saying that it's sorcery," I tell him.

"There, you see? What do they need to listen to Agretta for?"

"They're going to look, to see his condition. To judge his chances."

"They're not fools."

It's what the spectators at the library are doing, too, I realize—ignoring Chiesa's meretricious performance and studying his skin, his eyes. They've gone for the heart of the matter, what the body says will be.

Irritably, Chiesa searches his pockets for a cigarette, comes up empty-handed. "Well, go on then!" he flares at me. "Go perch in via Principe with all those other carrion-birds. All you'll gain from it is even more credulity, *Professoressa*— the kind of thing that makes you hate yourself. And afterwards we'll sit down together, the two of us—and we'll be just alike."

But I go anyway, because in the end I want to.

The *Palazzo* Grado is a heavy piece of whimsy misplaced on via Principe; its broad face rests its limestone chin right on the street, those paired staircases twisting down like moustaches to the pavement. The house belongs out in the countryside, with a crescent drive and high wrought-iron gates, topiary masking its face; here all its comings and goings have the cheap cachet of street theater, because anyone can see them.

When I arrive a late afternoon sun is slanting low and hard across the palazzo's face, orange as flame. A crowd has gathered in the combustible air, men and a few women— wives who've begged their husbands to escort them, widows who have simply buried their oppressive men and now go where they wish. Several aged Mercedes sedans arrive, carrying old barons and baronesses in rusty evening dress who lean heavily on their drivers' arms. The women all wear antique fur pieces, glass-eyed foxes biting each other's tails. Then businessmen and their sleek wives arrive, heavy guys in dark suits and sunglasses who drive their big BMWs up onto the curbs and leave them there. A priest shows up, breezy and smiling in his cassock—he's the third son of a well-connected family, I hear, and wears the cloth lightly. An editor, a *professore*, several Council members and municipal department heads show up on foot and mount the marble staircases.

We all wait for the mayor. He's late—late enough for the *Cavalière* himself to step out on the balcony and show us his displeasure: an abstracted, florid face above a wing collar and a red embroidered sash. All of us in the street understand that we are witnessing a drama, one whose actors will be good enough to signal us its offstage action. We shade our eyes against that occult sun and peer upward as the balcony shutters close.

Agretta arrives at last, but like a kidnap victim, not a partygoer. He's sprawled grey-faced in the passenger seat of a five-year-old Peugeot, and his wife has brought him here. It's her car, in fact—there are children's toys in the back seat and a woman's detritus on the dash, sunglasses, a printed silk scarf, a bottle of clear nail polish.

Right now, though, Signora Agretta is neither mother nor wife. She wrenches up the parking brake and exits the car like a force, showing a sprinter's calves. If it's her husband who has made her bring him here against her wishes I can't see it—there's nothing in her face but purpose. Agretta gapes behind the glass of the car window, following her with his eyes. He needs her to open the Peugeot's door for him.

We can all see at once the gravity of his illness. It makes us wish that we could look away, but we can't—we glance down the street for a moment's relief, and then we turn back.

He's dragged himself from the car's interior without a word to his wife. It's all he can manage for now, this transfer of his failing body from car seat to pavement on tottering legs. She reaches for his arm but he twitches it away, and neither of them lets on that he's done it deliberately. Now I know that this is what he wanted, to come here, and that she has only traded her own useless wishes for his more potent ones. It's a terrible forbearance that I see her exercising now, as she refuses to acknowledge the humiliation he's brought on her by showing himself like this.

Agretta shakes off his wife and creeps up those sweeping stairs, leaning heavily against the stone balustrade, careless of his white suit. On the high front terrace he turns to face us below him but he seems disoriented, unsure of how high he has climbed and what the glaring depth before him holds. He mops his face with a handkerchief; his shirt is dark with sweat and spilled water. He takes a deep, shuddering breath, then another, presses the handkerchief to his mouth. He has nearly steadied himself, I think, nearly quelled his nausea enough to speak to us.

It remains our most ardent wish—he begins, but the action of speech betrays him; it's too much like vomiting, his throat opening and his diaphragm pressing upward, and as we watch he chokes, his speech attenuates, distorts; his face takes on that gargoyle strain and he retches violently once, twice before bringing up a thick black arc of vomit that spatters richly, defacing the marble stairs. It could not be worse, like witnessing a disembowelling that leaves the victim alive and staring, and all of us left to overcome the horror and uncertainty of what to do with the intestines spilled on the floor. For an instant we all think that we might die of embarrassment; we wish we could. It's Agretta who saves us by collapsing, sinking to his knees and falling gracefully sideways,

the way actresses are taught to faint onstage. Men rush from
the *Cavalière*'s shuttered salon and fall upon him; the mayor's
wife puts her back against the dusty Peugeot like a witness
to an assault. I make for home like everyone else. We've seen enough,
we've gotten what we came for. When I return to the Elimo
the lobby is empty, the desk abandoned; on the stairs the
Guerrièra, armed for war, smiles like the sun.

In my rooms I lock the door, pull the curtains. Chiesa
will come if he sees a light on and so I sit motionless in the
dark, afraid to stir, as if he had a moth's hearing as well as
its propensity for light. I don't want to see him. There's a
sudden glare illuminating us both, it seems, light from the
mayor burning up.

I fear for Mayor Agretta. His jaunty suits and worldly
ambitions will not save him, no matter how he invokes their
imagined power. In the end they are just another set of
charms to him, more trash to clutch and prayers to whisper
against the things he never stopped believing. Agretta's sick
and getting sicker; he never did convert to skepticism.

Much later I wake in my chair to find the light on, Chiesa
drawn up in a chair before me, our knees touching. It's that
deep, uninhabited hour of the night, a darkness that echoes
like a cave. I sit up weakly, though I should be startled; I
don't know how he got into my rooms, or why the lamp is
on when I know that he will only beat himself against it. I
dread the damage he will do himself.

He speaks in long unbroken sentences, and this is the
protracted, exhausting flight that will undo him, all these
words: he tells me there's a bibliomane about, stealing old

military treatises from the library's stacks; he tells me that Rome has sent a new judge to Palermo to preside over the trials of the *mafiosi*, that a red imp was caught in a rabbit trap in Lenzi, that a friend of his, a *benandante*, has drawn a spell out of a woman like a splinter.

As he makes these indiscriminate reports to me his voice breaks—they are a confession, an admission of his culpability; he can disbelieve none of them. In his wretchedness he puts a cold palm to my cheek, presses his lips to mine. His eyes are like the windows of a darkened house.

CHAPTER FOURTEEN

In the archives I crack books open like shale and discard them; I go into the stacks on vague errands and stand there at a loss, waiting for the reason I'm there to come to me.

I'm not looking for books. If I were, I might just as well go to the fossil beds at Calatafimi and pick up bones and teeth.

My mother left Palermo every year around this time, in mid-July. She left in a rage, as if exiting a lovers' quarrel. She'd throw underwear, jewelry and a few wadded shifts into a small valise, leave the apartment key with an unwilling neighbor. *Come on, cara, let's get out of here,* she'd say to me, slamming doors. *What do they think—that the saint will excuse the blood in our streets? That anyone could intercede for us? Hypocrites! It's enough to make a pig cry!*

Out on the Corso wooden arches were going up over the street, stuck with tissue flowers and metallic paper and strung with colored lights. The *Festino* was on then, the streets jammed with tourists and country newlyweds come to see a tractor pull Santa Rosalia down the Corso on her mammoth barge. Already you could tell the city was going to lose hold of the celebration again this year, that events would run to chaos. The police recruits brought up to man the festival were watching girls' skirts; traffic had been routed down dead ends. Roma children in cast-off clothes harried the crowd like dogs after sheep, tugging, wheedling, robbing the unwary. We fled the gridlocked city, and the spectacle of the giant fiberglass *Santuzza* tearing balconies away in its progress through the streets. It felt like we were quitting the field, but in fact we were only travelling to another contested front: at the train station we boarded a *diretto* to Caltanisetta, and from there a bus to Aidone.

For the six days of the *Festino*, by agreement, my mother and her estranged family waged their perennial war with each other at the farmhouse in Aidone: endless rounds of shouted recriminations and arctic silences, deliberate slights and escalating cruelties. Every year it was the same. I'd leave them to it, walk down the good paved road that ran by the farm until it faded to a stone track, to the smashed Punic city of Morgantina, where Russell had dug that first summer he came to Sicily. The grass was dead of thirst by then, thickets had gone woody and aromatic; sheep stood on the flanks of brown hills, seeming to study the ground in their grazing. Their distant bells sounded like water in grottoes.

Another American team would be working there, from a different university—slab-chested boys in cut-offs with their hair grown out, jumping in and out of test pits; tanned blonde girls screening backdirt who'd smile at me and try to make friends. They spoke Italian like babies, but spoke to me as if I were the baby; I glared at them as if they were monsters, never let on that I spoke a broken English, rusty from summer's disuse. They watched helplessly as I ducked under ropes, stepped through grid strings, made outrageous

120

incursions into their work sites. I pretended to understand nothing.

The scale of ruin there at Morgantina—its desolate, consoling beauty—infuriated me. Fluted columns lay in sections on the ground like giant vertebrae; weeds burst through the floors and shattered walls of stoae, granaries, the bouleuterion, a fountain house. On a ridge above the agora, broken mosaics and the stumps of modest peristyles stood in the long grass. It was complex, beautiful, deceptively complete; whole lifetimes could be spent among the ruins of Morgantina.

Consoled by the vast wreckage that remained for them to sift and catalogue, those smiling college students never thought to mourn all that had been lost there.

CHAPTER FIFTEEN

The summer water shortages have begun, earlier than I remember them. You turn the faucets on in the afternoon and hear a faint sound of wind, a ventilating sigh. It makes you want to scream, that empty breath. I think of those excitable Sicilian marquises who built sirocco rooms in their villas to keep from going mad, to keep the wind out of their ears.

There is no water to be spared to hose down Valparuta's crusted, sulfurous streets. The work of the furious horde dries hard, cracks and warps like mud, takes on the filthy colors of industrial waste. The *Valparuti* pick their way through the stretches of poisonous slag without expression; they won't admit they've brought it on themselves. The vocal protests of a few, the wooly schemes to divert the town's grey water to the streets or pry the tarry masses up with paving tools are met with indifference and suspicion. No one speaks of *ripristino* anymore. The *Commissione* has passed all its funding to frontmen and sycophants and taken its kickbacks; meetings have ceased, its members can't be reached for comment. They've all gone to their sirocco rooms, perhaps.

Mayor Agretta has taken to his bed again, and no one expects him to rise from it this time. No statements issue from his home. The *Valparuti*, undeterred, make their own pronouncements.

That mago *has planted an old car inside him*, I hear a hen-naed sparrow of a woman tell her companion at the *paneficio*. It's late morning; the bread for lunch has just come from the oven, tipped from blackened trays into the bakery case. I've come for a few slender, honey-filled *nucatoli*, thinking Chiesa might eat them—they're insubstantial as the cigarettes he consumes in numbers but slightly curved, like little basking snakes, a shape that wakes your appetite. Outside, the day is already lost in a white glare, flowering plants fallen prostrate on stairs and balconies.

My heart thuds in my chest. The loaves of *rustico* look like a heap of dusty rubble in the bakery case; everyone presses forward.

This car is growing in him like a cancer, the woman says, poking coins up out of her change purse. *There's metal under his skin, his belly is full of crankcase oil. This is what my Ciccio says.*

Eh, marrône, *what a blunder!* her companion groans. *What will the Signora do?* She pinches the air with her fingers, signalling for a loaf.

I leave the bakery in a rush, the counter-woman calling after me cajolingly, thinking that I've taken some offense. But it's the air itself that's grown intolerable, its inescapable freight of sound and light.

Didn't Simona tear me out of her heart, didn't she send me off in Russell's insensible hands to make me a stranger to all this? Didn't she wish me my father's contempt for her people's tattling, oracular ignorance, their hankering after misfortune? I came here for the archives but I can raise nothing from them; instead it's the virulent dreams of others that are conjuring wraiths, lights, voices out of me, as if I were the haunted scene of some old tragedy and not the handful of fragment-laden earth I know myself to be.

I hear Chiesa on the hotel stairs, climbing slowly up to his rooms. I think of him there above me in the evening hours, eating couscous and fish broth—invalid's food—and reading the day's *La Sera*, a useless exercise. He washes the cookpot with a rag wrapped round a splinter of bath soap, sleeves rolled to his forearms, cigarette in his lips. I have this knack for calling up what people have done for centuries in rooms, and I use it now just as I would for one long dead, someone I never knew. Chiesa startles up from the dull book he's reading. He has nearly fallen asleep in his chair; the brass floor lamp behind him has a brown silk shade, and he has turned a tear in it to the wall.

He does not suffer bouts of hopelessness in these evenings, he does not have sudden difficulty breathing. He undresses at the side of his bed, there is no closet; he has four suits and a black silk cutaway coat for funerals in an enormous rosewood armoire, and an old beechwood clothes butler that catches his trousers and shirt. In the drawer of his night table there are vials labelled *diazepina* and a glass-barrelled syringe, and in lamplight at the very end of his day he inspects the discreet puncture wounds on the insides of his elbows.

Pastries will do nothing for Chiesa. He needs something *ex machina* to pluck him up out of our midst and carry him off to safety; there's no possibility of amending him so that he might save himself. The days stretch out in a long, languid voyage through strange waters, sunlight lancing off the dome of the *chiesa matrice*. We are becalmed, all of us. It's the depths beneath us that are moving, teeming with dark shapes.

Morning once again, and I'm at Chiesa's desk in the archives, staring like a bystander at the heap of furniture and personal effects rescued from a burning house in 1558. The assiduous neighbors have risked singed hair and blistered palms, carrying out blackened chairs and earthenware while the owner lay dead inside, her bed a pyre. I've fixed my thoughts on this spectacle and the value back then of things utilitarian, each object difficult to replace and unique as a life. In the back of my mind, held at bay there, the mayor's eyes leak green coolant, the skin of his back splits over sheet metal.

The phone on the desk shrills once, twice; I seize the handset as if it were my racing heart, to still it.

The library is closed for the remainder of the day, Professoressa. In the background I hear the thump of a stapler—it's Chiesa with the phone trapped between shoulder and ear and both hands free, multitasking to no purpose. *I'll let you out.*

I can't account for my dismay. For weeks now I've watched the scenes formed by my lists of objects without expectation; they're nothing but distraction now, to keep my mind from darker, more florid imaginings. But surely I can find something else to occupy me for a day—a long walk if nothing else, or some hours spent organizing useless data, the hard work of feigning purpose. So why this sudden flight of panic?

"You can't just—"

But of course I can. My continued presence here defies all odds; all bets are off. I'll do just as I please.

"Where are you going?"

The musical rustle of thin pages turned quickly, as if he's searching a glossary for his answer. *A collector has asked me to consult on a recent acquisition. In Alcamo.*

An hour's ride or more from Valparuta, depending on the route he chooses.

"Something worth the trip, you think."

I don't know, Professoressa. *This gentleman was* molto astuto *on the phone, very cagey. He didn't want to say.*

More sounds of Chiesa's divided attention, the scrape of a chair, footfalls. He's in a hurry; he suspects this collector of something. But when he speaks he sounds only matter-of-fact.

You might enjoy the ride.

"And this item he's acquired?"

You might enjoy that, too.

I listen to him moving, pacing, putting his desk in order. I hear the hollow sound of fabric against the phone, monstrously amplified; he's pulling on his suitcoat one-handed, fumbling the phone.

"You're thinking you might need a witness."

For a moment there's nothing but the confused sounds of his haste.

Come with me, he says.

He's tried to buy off his conscience with this car of his, an immense Lancia the color of glittering sand. The compartment chimes discreetly when he opens the car door, revealing buttoned leather seats and a veneered dash. The interior is underwater-dim, the weather perpetually lowering through tinted windows. We travel at a strange remove from the landscape around us, a distance I would have thought Sicily's broken roads and sweeping vistas would not have permitted. The insistent sun, the heat retreats before us.

The car, ponderous and stable as an airliner, descends Valparuta's bluff on a steep switchbacked road, the vertical drop below thick with the crowns of trees. On the cluttered outskirts of Trapani Chiesa chooses the huge raised

A29 superstrada, pushes the car to 140 as soon as he's cleared the entrance ramp. I can't feel our hurtling speed—I only see it like a movie as we overtake a line of cars, seemingly travelling at the dignified pace of a cortege. But we're all speeding. The land rises into vast dry hills of eroded limestone.

"This is hardly a librarian's car, Signor Chiesa." I'm cool as I've been in weeks; the Lancia's air conditioning gives me a feeling of self-possession that I should not trust.

Chiesa shoots me a thin, deprecating smile. He has a stunt driver's ease at the wheel, gripping it lightly, his arms extended. "This fellow will know me," he says.

"You've seen his collection?"

Chiesa nods. "More gourmand than connoisseur, *Professoressa*—you're unlikely to be impressed." We drive for a while in silence. "As for the car," he says, "I've lost my fondness for it."

He doesn't have to tell me that he's sunk his extravagant salary into it, trying to enjoy the fruits of his extortion. "You've never liked it," I say.

He stares hard at the road. "Not really, no."

"You should have known, Chiesa. You know yourself well enough."

"And you?"

"Me?"

"Have you stopped trying to do like everyone else? Knowing yourself so well?"

I think of my failed string of teaching posts, my unhappy efforts to conform.

Chiesa nods. "We think it should be easy, a welcome relief—yes? But it's not."

"You presume a great deal, Signor Chiesa."

He won't even reply to this. He lights a cigarette, and we plunge into a long, unlit tunnel; in the near blackness I can feel him studying me. When we emerge from the mountain's side the hills are closer, steeper, streaked with pale falls of scree. The road shimmers in the heat.

He's allowing me perspective, I realize, bringing me out here on this giant, thinly-travelled highway in his anomalous car; he's offering a deeper look. It's a disarming gesture—he knows by now that I see readily. And so I let my eyes take in the parched, dramatic landscape, the worn-down bulk of hills and distant plains. Lone farmhouses rest in the shallow folds of fields, a few tended trees nearby.

"What will you do without the library, Chiesa?"

He sighs. "I don't know. When I try to look ahead it's dark—like these tunnels." He smiles to make a joke of it.

"But tunnels end."

"Perhaps the metaphor doesn't extend that far, *Professoressa*."

I press a hand to my forehead, shield my eyes from the sky's muted, grey-green glare. He can't see it, is what he's saying—he can't see what he'll do.

These hazy, desolate vistas; the twitch and flattening of brown grasses in the Lancia's violent wake. Chiesa has thrown away every last centime he owned, buying this car. I know he has; I see it. He is saving for nothing—not a holiday, a television, a stereo system, a villa—and he is not saving for a wife. He has no more expectations. The car is a cashing-out, a liquidation of hopes.

"I wish you'd stayed up north," I say.

He laughs. "The damned trains bring us back."

"They bring back the factory workers. Not you."

"I always intended to return, *Professoressa*. I went away to university so that I could come back."

To what, I wonder? He'd carried the night battles abroad with him like an infection, with no chance for nostalgia;

and he must have known that Sicily would grind away the honed edges university gave him.

"You were waiting for this post."

He downshifts expertly, swings the Lancia out to pass another line of cars. "I meant to have it, yes. But I didn't just wait. There was other work—a cataloguing project in Bari, water damage assessment in Trapani . . . that sort of thing. Some work in private collections."

"How long?"

He doesn't want to tell me. "Nine years."

It's too long, too long to wait for anything—and so poorly consoled in the meantime. I see him there in dreary, modern Trapani, an archivist's purgatory; he's bending over a stack of incunabula that have been unsympathetically rebound in tightbacked morocco and so have survived their wetting badly. The librarian blames Chiesa for how little can be done for them, agitates for his departure. He moves on in a few months, casting about for something to occupy his hands, his mind.

For nine years.

Another lightless tunnel, another long moment like sleep. And something happens there that opens a door, something involuntary that the darkness at once permits and conspires to hide. Chiesa lays the back of his hand against my face. I smell the cigarettes on his fingers and something sweeter, the minimal care he still affords himself. He has the wheel in both hands again when we emerge into daylight. It's as if he's flung his arm out like a sleeper, intentionless—but he's passed his ferocious longing to me like a code.

And all at once I understand. Nine years was too long to wait, even for Valparuta's archives. There'd been something else at stake.

129

His fiancée. The woman whose tongue he boxed like a velvet ribbon in his sleep.

I've learned my lesson; I don't interrogate him. Instead I lie back in the deep leather seat, let myself feel nothing but the residual firing of nerves where he touched my face. We travel like strangers sharing a train compartment, granting the other a thin formal privacy by looking away, by pretending that nothing has happened. Behind us the unfinished temple at Segesta stands on an eminence marred by the tunnel we've just exited.

After a while I stir myself up to contend with the silence between us.

"Who do you think is stealing your military treatises, then?"

He looks at me sharply; the car veers like a skittish horse. "Who told you?"

"You did—hold the road, Chiesa!"

He stares ahead intently but he's oversteering now, the car feinting toward the highway's concrete divider. "I've told no one."

"But you—"

"I've told no one!" he shouts.

An exit flashes up; Chiesa veers hard toward it, the car nearly weightless as it takes the ramp. I brace a palm against the roof, consider the short deadly flight down the embankment to rocks and scrub. But the brakes shudder us down to speed, groaning mightily.

Chiesa drives the car into gravel and sparse crested grass, throws it out of gear. He puts his face close to mine. "Has the Council been talking to you?"

"No. You told me."

"*When* did I tell you this?"

"Get out of my face," I say.

He sits back hard against the car door. "When?"

"The night of *Cavalière* Grado's fucking soiree."

"No."

"Chiesa, you came to my rooms—"

But as I say it I know I'm wrong; I should have tried it aloud sooner, this claim of mine, even on my own ears. Because it sounds ridiculous to me now: *You came to my rooms. Through a locked door.*

I get out. A stiff wind carries heat and grit from the road into my face, draws a long minor note from the tall weeds. We've come down in a broad valley, complicated interchanges and the superstrada's colossal footings disrupting the vineyards on its slopes. The shriek of high-speed travel overhead threatens more violence.

Chiesa stands beside me against the car. He's put on dark glasses; his tie flutters out from his body. He leans in to me to keep the wind from carrying off his words, to avoid having to shout to weight them down.

"Are you so lacking in discernment, *Professoressa?*" he says. "Can you not distinguish dream from waking?"

Furious, chagrined, I strain away from him like a dog tied to a stake. "Don't bait me, you hypocrite—"

"It's just a question, *Professoressa.*"

"If I'd mentioned it to anyone, if I'd just said it aloud before this, I'd have known."

"No doubt."

"I knew as soon as I—"

"All right."

The gravel gives way under my feet; a tractor trailer loaded with construction brick thunders by overhead, displacing huge, concussive walls of air. Chiesa is still standing next to me, leaning against the car. He thinks he's taught me a lesson, something about *omerta*.

I hit him hard in the chest.

He takes the blow with a small pained noise, his back thumping hard against the car, but I haven't hurt him or even put him off much.

"Fuck you, Chiesa, *fuck* you—" For some reason I'm the one who's having trouble breathing. "Do you think I'm stupid? Do you think I can't see for myself? I don't need your damned *object lessons*—I get what silence does! So it holds things in limbo, it leaves experience unsorted. Who gives a fuck? What about the bibliomane?"

He appeals mutely to the air, at a loss. "What about it?"

"There *is* a bibliomane!"

"Several pamphlets have gone missing, yes."

"But you told me in a *dream!*"

"Not me. Not me."

"Then how the fuck did I *know?*"

He's trying to rub the ache out of his chest with the heel of his hand. "Why is this hard, *Professoressa?*" he says. "You have insight, that's all. Didn't you know?"

I walk away from him then, away from the idling car and out into the thin grass. Bits of rubber and safety glass fleck the balding ground; the heat comes from the fallow graded slope and not the sky at all.

I know what he's saying. There they are, the *benandanti*, their secret wriggling out of their mouths like a fish from hands—they can't hold onto it, despite the beatings lined up for them, a formidable deterrence. They want to speak. They need the uncomprehending stares of their listeners, the corroborations, contradictions, refinements, denunciations and interrogations that come back to them when they do; it's their sonar, their only means of mapping a psychic terrain complex as a sunken coast. This is the point Chiesa wants to make. Precognition? The thing that has me trying to flee my own shadow, jump out of my skin? It's nothing—a sharp set of eyes.

Chiesa perseveres, speaks up behind me. "It's only rustics and catalepts, *Professoressa*, who conflate dreams with waking."

I turn back to take him in at a distance; it's what he's brought me out here for, after all. He stands with the car like an apparition, overdressed, his eyes hidden, the steady wind pressing his clothes against his body. The wind might pick him up and whirl him to fragments at any moment, it seems—or he might be made of iron, indestructible, a weight and a warning.

"*Ma che m'importa?*" I hear my voice shrill and fall like all the angry, thwarted *donne* I've ever heard. "What do I care which is which? Your bibliomane doesn't!"

"Then you're no better than the dog who wakes up from a twitching sleep and goes looking for the thing it chased in its dreams."

"You saw crickets in stairwells, Chiesa. Who are you to say?"

A black length of thrown tread sails off the overpass, flexing; it lands without sound in the weeds. Chiesa looks away, out toward the rows of dust-laden vines set in bricky earth. Out here and in this light anyone could see there's something wrong with him, standing there thin and beetle-dark on the road's negligible shoulder. I thought his bottled, caviling contempt was aimed at me, but it's not; he would erase himself if he could, like an aberration.

"You take my point," he says.

CHAPTER SIXTEEN

On the edge of Alcamo, among the scattered reclaimed shacks of the local *mezzadri*, we pass a knot of people in the road. They shuffle out of the Lancia's path on stiffened legs and turn to stare, draggled children in ankle-deep dust sucking their fingers, men and women with weathered, perennially crestfallen faces. They've forgotten themselves in their distress, forgotten even their bodies and what to do with them; they stand listing, an arm thrown over a head, hands hanging, their legs graceless props. There's no sign of what concerns them. Wandering lines of piled stone and rusting wire fence mark small, intensively-cultivated plots of eggplant and tomatoes, melons and citrus trees; blackberry canes arc out into the road. A mongrel chained to a pipe barks soundlessly—and I see now where journalists in war zones get those tilted shots of frozen people in a middle distance with nothing but sky behind them: they're taken from the relative safety of cars, through rolled-up windows. One man steps forward to offer commentary, belatedly and without conviction, but Chiesa doesn't stop.

"What's this?"

Chiesa shakes his head; we haven't spoken in miles. He's saying wait, you'll know soon enough.

Even without the broad, many-footed stain in the road I'd have known it for the scene of a killing. There's an old wellhead set in a wide turnout, a big stone affair with a diesel pump sunk in its concrete cap. The door of the nearby caretaker's shed stands open onto its disordered contents, a tipped chair, scattered tools. The whole place has the dilapidated, off-season look of a busy enterprise suddenly abandoned.

The stain's creeping peninsulas have undermined the road dust, carried it along glittering on its dark advance before subsiding into the earth.

"That's heart blood." I've said it before I can stop myself.

Chiesa looks at me sharply. "What?"

I pretend not to hear, crane around in my seat to keep my back to him. The scene recedes, masked by roadside overgrowth, but I continue to stare after it to hide my face from Chiesa.

This connoisseurship of blood, forensic and morbid all at once—my mother's legacy again. These aptitudes that continue to surprise and unnerve me. But even a black and white photograph conveys it, the thick, gallon-sized spill— like paint from a tipped can—that results when the torn heart pumps itself dry on the ground. It's the pool of blood you lie in that makes the uninitiated whisper, *Where does it all come from?* And then there's the smell, salt, faintly tidal, the mouth of a wet iron pipe.

"It's nothing," I tell Chiesa, too late to forestall anything. But he lets the moment pass, palming the wheel through a tight curve. His absorption in the road is tactful only, not genuine; I see the tiny smile of effort it costs him.

The collector's home stands well back in a dark lemon grove, a tall Bourbonesque villa the color of faded velvet, hung with iron balconies and an excess of pitted stone festoons. Chiesa has taken a leather briefcase from the car's back seat; now he peers into the villa's security camera, speaks, and the barred gate trundles aside for us. The compound's walls are covered in ivy and bougainvillea and topped with broken glass; the gate locks behind us with a violent, monitory buzz. I walk with him across a terrace littered with strings of fallen mimosa blossoms; a stone fish stands on its tail in a basin of papyrus, spouting water.

"Let him think that you are my associate," Chiesa says as we reach the villa's ironbound door. "Signor Masuccio is anxious to unburden himself."

But it does not seem so to me.

He greets us himself, Signor Masuccio, dragging the great door ajar just enough to admit us—a beaming, slightly infirm old man in evening dress and black patent opera slippers. He holds his delight at seeing us in clasped hands against his chest, wringing them softly, pleasurably. Vases of withered flowers stand on the pier tables behind him; old odors have come out of the walls.

Chiesa shakes the old man's fingers like a godson, dutiful and condescending. I am his colleague, Chiesa says, a respected American bibliographer consulting in the archives. He tells this lie easily.

Signor Masuccio folds himself over my hand.

He has sent his wife and his unmarried daughters to Marina, he tells us, but not why; his man Bartolomeo is out patrolling the fences. He leads us through a series of rooms set like still lifes, artful jumbles of furniture, plates and draperies, potted palms and Turkish rugs just beginning to dull with dust. "We'll have a drink after," he says. "I've set the book out in the library—it's cooler there."

Chiesa takes in the clutter, the stale air. He's making notes toward a conclusion that does not please him.

"Where did you—?" he says.

"A bookdealer in Catania!" Signor Masuccio cries. "Of all places! This gentleman had offered me items before, nothing I fancied. His name has escaped me, isn't that strange? An old man's mind—"

He shakes his head in mock despair. A cat has delivered a gecko's limbless body to the threshold of the library, where it's been left to lie.

I'm expecting some big gaudy volume got up in false bands and full leather, a French philosophical treatise or an odd single from some royal's library with gold-stamped heraldry on its covers. But the book on the corner of Signor Masuccio's library table is no bigger than my hand, a thick little volume in leather gone black with age.

Chiesa won't touch it.

"*Professoressa?*" he says. He's busy opening his briefcase; he wants me incriminated first.

I wipe my fingers on my thighs, lift the book. I know at once that it is very, very old—a book with a fossil's extra weight, it seems, as if its cell walls have mineralized—but it's the weight of medieval craft I'm feeling, wooden boards, full-thickness goatskin and vellum text bound up with knotted thongs and horn glue. Cords have been laid down in spirals on the upper board, under the leather covering, to form a raised design; the lower covering is blind tooled in a diamond pattern.

I open it just to be sure it's what I think it is, set it back on the table. Something like black snow is falling at the edges of the room; there's a sick, cold tingle in my hands and feet and face.

"*Professoressa?*" Chiesa says again.

Signor Masuccio shoots his cuffs, studies a bare wrist. "She's pleased, I think!" he says.

Chiesa waits, his brittle smile a warning.

"You are to be congratulated," I say at last. "It's a very fine acquisition."

Signor Masuccio, preening, consults his absent wrist-watch. "What do you make of it, then?" he says.

Chiesa turns to a long suit of identical bindings on the shelves behind him, touches his fingers idly along their headcaps. The lie he's told traps me; I can't claim ignorance or even much uncertainty.

I tell him it's Northumbrian, a seventh or eighth century text and binding. I'm hoping the old man will leave it at that, but he doesn't.

"And the text?" he says. "What is it?"

Chiesa has taken down one of those matching books they sell by the linear foot; he pretends not to hear.

"One of the gospels," I say.

Signor Masuccio waits. Something has come to the surface in him, a reptilian glint; a slow pulse shows under the pebbly skin of his neck. He knows exactly what he has. But I tell him anyway, with a bibliographer's false hedging:

"I believe it's St. John."

Signor Masuccio offers to bring us *tè freddo*, takes the air with him from the room.

I think about setting the library's velvet drapes on fire. "You know what it is," I say.

Chiesa sits on the edge of the table, the little pocket gospel between us. He has not touched it.

"Do you think those orange-faced Jesuits should see their book again?" he says.

"What kind of question is that?"

"It's been thirty years, *Professoressa*. They couldn't even say exactly when it had been taken."

I leave him, leave the book. Through the library windows' tiny, flawed panes I see a man's distorted shape—Bartolomeo coming back from his patrol. There's a shotgun in the crook of his arm.

Every student of library science, every frequenter of archives knows this story: an Irish saint's book, an object of immense cultural and artifactual value, is taken from the rare book room of a small Jesuit college in Hexham. The vitrine lock is picked; the heavy cube of Plexiglas is tipped and the book removed, a cheap black missal set in its place. It happens during library hours. Staff is in the room but back in the stacks, maybe, away from the desk or somehow heedless; it's a student browsing the display—who knows how much later—who finally asks if it's a joke, a flimsy New Word missal in the Cadmus Gospel's place.

Thirty years ago.

It's been travelling among Europe's less principled dealers and collectors for a while, I'd guess, to end up here in Signor Masuccio's hands; he has no understanding of what he's acquired, just a mercenary's fondness for the trappings of high culture, a wish to legitimate himself.

"He misses his daughters, I think," Chiesa says. "They never seem to tire of overpraising his successes."

"Bartolomeo is carrying a gun."

"Then it's no time to have the women about, is it?"

Outside, Bartolomeo has stopped to slap dust from his boots. He stares at the house as if it has defeated him, as if he knows that he will never get away.

"These are more than just clients to you."

"No. I am more than an appraiser to them. The daughters—"
He attempts a description with his hands but gives up; his
smile is rueful, complacent.

I can just see it, and God help me but it is funny: two
or three spoiled, querulous women just out of their looks,
twined about the archivist like cats. They've just woken to
the fact that their aging father has betrayed them; they've
earned exactly nothing for their years of calculated worship.
From moment to moment Chiesa can't be sure whether the
sisters will coddle or dismember him.

He stands, pushes his hands deep in his pockets. "They
take after their father," he says. "Their considerable refinements don't quite hide the souls of pirates."

"We haven't seen the black flag yet."

"He'll run it up if this goes badly."

"Well, what does he expect? He's gone and bought a
major art theft—"

"He is a man of honor, *Professoressa*. He expects that
there will be no trouble, no awkward questions."

"He'll be disappointed, then."

Chiesa reaches me in two long strides. "I don't intend to
disappoint him. Do you?"

"What are we here for, then? To take the place of his
admiring daughters?"

Chiesa shrugs. "He gives them what they want."

"He gives them what he wants to give them."

"And what do you think he wants with this book?"

Distant, raised voices reach us, the house's tiled halls dis-
torting the sound like blown amps: Signor Masuccio berating
Bartolomeo.

"He's acquisitive, the old martinet—a secret despoiler.
He wants to keep it," I say.

Chiesa shakes his head. "He wants to be rid of it, *Professoressa*. He would not have called me otherwise."

Off in the distant kitchen, Signor Masuccio breaks a plate to make his point.

And all at once I know that out of contempt for women's work and ignorance of all things domestic, Signor Masuccio has vandalized his wife's kitchen in her absence. He's laid down indelible wine stains on the counters, clogged the burners with charred food; he's blackened every saucepan in the house. He rants at Bartolomeo in the ruin he's created, the kitchen windows already flyblown.

"You saw that he knew the book," Chiesa says.

"He doesn't know the book! All he knows is what someone would pay for it—it's a piece of illegal treasure to him, something to wave under our noses."

Chiesa shades his eyes, stares out at the vine-choked wall, the thick sky. "If his women were at home and the house were in order—if Bartolomeo weren't carrying a gun—I would say yes, you're right. But something has gone badly wrong here, it's thrown the old man out of himself. Signor Masuccio sees other reasons, other meanings for things now."

Silence from the kitchen. I ask Chiesa how he knows this.

"That well we passed? It belongs to the Masuccio." His hands fall; he studies his palms. "No one will dare buy water from them now."

"That blood—"

"But for you I'd have taken it for oil." He wishes that I hadn't told him. "There was an elderly caretaker who administered the Masuccio's water rights," he says. "I think he has been killed."

I look hard into Chiesa's face. The bent, spotted light coming through the window's old glass throws blemishes over his skin.

"Someone is working to supplant the Masuccio," I say.

"The Masuccio are an old family, *Professoressa*, they've grown complacent. Others have come up who are more ambitious."

There's that instinctive circumlocution again, the coded deflection of meaning. For decades no one in Sicily said *Mafia* except to deny its existence.

Chiesa leaves the window and the sun's harsh measure of his health. "The book is a judgment visited upon him, *Professoressa*," he says. "He wishes to be rid of it."

Chapter Seventeen

I was seeing what lay around corners and down long hall-ways—wasn't I? I'd taken in those tawny, faded upland vistas where distance stilled all motion and a curtain hung over the horizon. I had sight. Why didn't I see, then, the subtle apprenticeship Chiesa worked to bring me to that afternoon? I could smell didacticism a mile off, it stank to heaven to my nose; I missed it entirely on Chiesa. All I saw in him was the creeping, painful zealousness of the recently reformed—that and an addict's self-loathing. I didn't see that he was making an example of himself.

What curtailed my view?

I'll tell you two things:

Chiesa, like it or not, was of the *benandanti*. He could move the seen and the unseen like magician's cards.

And I—I was ignorant and visionary as those girls leaning over a basin of water in my mother's apartment. I could be led a certain distance.

The sugar lies in billows at the bottoms of our glasses. Signor Masuccio potters with the dripping tray, playing at serving us, pleased to watch us drink from dirty glasses and suffer his elaborate incompetence.

The afternoon does not go well.

Perhaps the Professoressa *would prefer to wait in the car,* Chiesa finally says to me, glaring. I've just told a long, meretricious tale of an imaginary bibliomane who's been plaguing the university where I'm supposedly tenured—a mad Pakistani autodidact who'd crammed his dorm room with seven thousand stolen books.

Signor Masuccio has developed a coarse Parkinsonian tremor, his head bobbling like a balloon on the stem of his neck.

So I leave, I walk away from their derailed complicity. The truncated gecko on the threshold is still alive, its tiny sides furling like bellows.

Chiesa has put the Lancia's keys in the folded sun visor. Did he really think that I'd just sit and wait for him?

I speed through a changed landscape, alone this time. It's the invisible sea's domain now, stacked lances of palmetto in salt-white sand, a hardened sky. The women have all been sent to the beach at Marina to get them out of the way; I've quit the field in protest and now I'm useless, too, another liability best packed away in sand. The Lancia's transmission howls under my feet. I open the sunroof and feel my hair rise toward it, busy as snakes in the buffeting vacuum.

I think I'm turning into something, I flatter myself that I am—but I'm no judge. Chiesa is the one who'd know.

Improbable flora appears in this new terrain, however: a giant carob, the elbows of its great black arms resting on the ground; aniline-green palms; lion-colored patches of broom. I gun the car toward the sea, its gear ratio a puzzle I can't be bothered with.

How long am I gone? An hour, maybe two? Long enough to use the Lancia's bulk and flash and magisterial horn to gain the clogged beach road; long enough to find the burning, littered, trampled sand unbearable, the flat white sea necessary and unlovely as the bucket of water in a blacksmith's forge—it's where you douse your red-hot self when the sun has hammered you flat. Hundreds of bathers lie side by side in the sand, blackened, rotund, clamoring; they lumber to the water like creatures who have lost their affinity for land. The air smells of food and chemical toilets.

The silk wrap I'm wearing as a skirt will do a lot of things, but it won't let me swim. I have to leave.

And on my way back to Chiesa's car I see them, clinging like castaways to the rail of a raised beach cabana: three women in dark *maillots* and Hermès headscarves, their makeup gone waxy in the heat. Their black designer sunglasses give them the faces of mantises, but I can still see worry in the corners of their mouths.

Marooned, discontented, what I think are the Masuccio women descend to the beach to tan.

In Alcamo it seems that I've been gone for days.

I can raise no one from the villa, no matter how I ring the gate and shout into the security camera's dead blue eye; smoke drifts from the back of the house. The kitchen has caught fire and is burning like a smudge pot—a lazy, harmless blaze whose whole purpose seems to be its oily, speaking smoke and not its flame at all.

Nothing remains behind to tell me whether this is arson or the old man's carelessness. What's happened here is gone, fugitive; there's just this unintelligible smoke saying either they're all dead inside—Bartolomeo sagging in a splintered doorway, Chiesa and Masuccio on the library floor, their blood on the walls—or the house has been left burning unattended like a candle, the men all at the station putting Chiesa on a train.

A hot breeze pulls its fingers through the neglected garden. It's so picturesque, this scene of abandonment, the blown roses and downed leaves, green water in a horse trough of grey tufa. Even the smoke seems contrived now, ingenious: *How did they do it?*

The gate holds me off at a spectator's distance.

It's as if I've just taken in one of those gaudy, ill-planned pageants you see everywhere in Sicily, old religious enthusiasms reduced to reflex: I'm left half-inspired, my amazement rapidly cooling. None of this—the dead caretaker, the stolen book, not even the burning villa—is meant to move my heart. I've only lost Chiesa in the smoke from the day's pyrotechnics; the small stony possibility that he's dead concerns me less than finding my way back to Valparuta alone.

My hands come away from the bars of the gate flecked with rust.

Trapani is where events begin to slide off into nightmare.

The western sun smolders down to white ash and I drive right into it, the Lancia's dusty windshield nearly opaque; two cicadas have broken like eggs on the glass in front of my face. I drive the car with no sense of husbandry, flogging it, sending it into potholes, burning the clutch, snarling the gears. It's a creature no one loves, a troublesome conveyance; I think I'd like to do it in as a favor to Chiesa. The long drive back on the A29 with the sun in my eyes hasn't cleared my thoughts.

But when the car quits on me, when the engine stops as if obeying a command on a long desolate feeder road outside of Trapani, it seems like certain justice. I pat the dashboard, say come on, come on now, but the car rolls into the weeds at the side of the road as if it intends to graze there. I turn the key and the starter whinnies and whinnies until I run the battery down. I think to lower the car windows before it dies completely, and then I sit there in the Lancia's rapidly heating interior, listening to the engine sigh and tick. The warming upholstery gives off the smell of Chiesa's cigarettes.

I've stalled in one of those extra-urban purgatories you see all over Sicily, a graveyard for public funds marked by empty access roads and half-built highrise apartments. They're an embarrassment, monuments to bureaucratic corruption and Mafia control; no one goes there. There's soccer graffiti on unfaced walls, weeds breaking up the concrete divider. A plastic shopping bag caught in a hedge swells like something poisonous.

The heat drives me out of the car before I know what I'm going to do. I stand on the road's crumbling edge with my fists in my hair but without the panic the gesture implies; I just want the weight off my neck. If someone were to strike my chest right now I think it would ring like a gong.

I find a stale half-pack of Chiesa's black cigarettes in the glove compartment, foil liner and box hastily torn open (there's Chiesa in a nicotine fit, punching the dashboard lighter, the car drifting toward the median), and I light one up, even though it will only make me thirstier. The smoke goes right to my head, a pleasant, remote sensation, like viewing a sky with high clouds.

So when the dark underpass on the opposite side of the road produces a tow truck, a glittering red emergency vehicle with polished sidewalls and a big chrome grille, I just feel that silly elation of one who sees her ass suddenly and undeservedly saved. I step into the road without thinking, my hand goes up—here, here!—and it's not until the truck has rocked up over the divider like a tank and swung toward me in a stiff curve that it occurs to me who this might be, coming from the direction of Valparuta in a truck still bearing the unnatural gleam of the showroom.

And it is. It's Risacca. *He has a certain rapport with cars*, Chiesa told me; I'd thought I was alone on the road all this time, but I wasn't.

What does the mechanic see that tells him a car is disabled, the long anonymous stretch of road where it's died? Are there windows onto all his vehicles in his head, his mind's eye moving like a lookout from one to the next?

I was singing loudly and off-key against my thoughts as I drove; I was talking to myself, moaning. I wiped my nose on the back of my hand, pulled my skirt up to cool my thighs. Did Risacca see this, too?

There's no getting away from him. The truck pulls up next to me in a rush of heat and fumes; the passenger window runs down.

"Get out of the way, *Professoressa!*" Risacca shouts. "I'll take it from here."

In the cab's dark interior he's an indistinct shape, a reflection in water. I want to shout at him *Take what? Take what from here?* But he'll only turn that black contempt he reserves

for foreign women on me and say *The car,* idiota, *the car!* He'd
never tell me what I think is true, that management of this
day's artifice has just passed from Chiesa's hands to his.
I step back onto the broken curb.
Risacca has already run the window up; the truck shifts
into gear with a roar, its oversized radiator fan sucking air
over the coils.

I never doubted that my mother got willingly into that government car with the *onorevole* Leoluca Dandi. She'd have
wanted to interview him, photograph him; she liked those
brief journalistic conquests, so much like a tussle under the
stairs. The emptied highway and the mirrored windshields of
their police escort would have figured in her portraits from
that day.

I think at some point every woman accepts a ride she
knows is dangerous. She wants to or she has no choice—or
she fails herself somehow, conspires in an unnecessary risk.

I get in with Risacca.

He knows better than to point out to me the obvious,
that I can't stay behind. I've already seen the stands of chap-
arral and dry gravel washes that declare the place a desert;
I'm already slightly distracted by thirst. He sets the iron tow
hook deep in the Lancia's undercarriage and takes possession
of the car without a word, his strange proprietary clairvoy-
ance evidence enough of his right to it. I leave him to it,
climb up onto the truck's bench seat before he can lay claim
to me, too.

The cab is clean, refrigerated, lit like a jukebox. There's
a half-liter of water on the seat in a reused San Pellegrino
bottle and I drink it, twisting the bottle's mouth in my fist

as a sort of useless exorcism—I still taste Risacca when I swallow. He's laminated prayer cards onto the dashboard, a dense collage of pierced, illuminated hearts, cherubim and colored robes; he's hung gold drapery fringe over the windshield. It's like a psychic's parlor in here, cool and dim, over-ornamented, a hint of marvels deliberately withheld. Outside, Risacca tends Chiesa's car as if it were a downed animal.

He climbs into the cab, a single trickle of sweat down his face. He shakes the gearshift, releases the floor brake; his thoughts are elsewhere.

"You've broken a front shock, *Professoressa*," he says, and the truck lunges, pulls up short. "The clutch is worn."

I still have that mangled pack of Chiesa's cigarettes. I put one between my lips. "Your cars break down too easily," I say.

"I told you as much, didn't I?"

"Yes. But you know I'm destructive, Signor Risacca."

He groans appreciatively. "Those gunpowder eyes—I smell it on you. I think you meant to summon me."

I shoot him a barbed, outraged look, take ostentatious note of the length of seat between us.

But who's to say that I didn't? I like this feeling that I'm closing with an adversary, that I'm free to do my worst.

Chiesa's car swims back and forth behind us in the tow truck's heavy wake.

Later, I'll confuse Risacca's garage with Villa Masuccio again and again. It will seem a kind of agnosia, a permanent defect of perception; no matter how I task myself I will never be able to sort out my impressions of those two places. There was a gate whose bars showed welded, discolored joints, another that was rusting through its paint; there were two walled compounds, two house facades and two ways in which the light fell over them. I will always conflate them. One was the shadow of the other, its inverse, I think—but both were dark.

Risacca lives above his garage, in a building whose unfinished state somehow ornaments it. Rebar protrudes from the foundation, mortar maps the walls. He must have a wife—laundry hangs from wires off the terrazzo railing—but I never see her. And he has children of a sort, two berserker kids not his own, apprenticed to his dubious work.

Those two close on me as soon as Risacca leaves the garage to phone his parts supplier.

They've been screwing around under a faded old BMW, riding car creepers on their bellies, hooting with laughter. Now they climb to their feet and sidle towards me, puffing a little, hot and grave with something that's not quite been play. They're not quite teenagers, either, I see; their scrubbed faces show the good effects of their mothers' coddling, and their newfound disdain for it.

"That your car?" asks the bigger of the two. He's tall, with arms and legs like tubes and a girl's neck.

"No," I say. "I stole it from a friend."

They laugh uproariously, clutching at each other. They can only ridicule a woman's enterprise, no matter how it may impress them; they're angry at me now for making them behave like idiots.

"He still your friend, that guy?" the other says.

"He wanted me to steal it."

This sets them off again, even more determinedly; they push each other to the floor, throw wild haymakers; it's all violence meant for me.

"He didn't want you to steal his car, lady!" the second boy crows. "He probably wants to fuck you or something, so he let you drive his car. You weren't supposed to steal it!"

This one has the orange, wooly hair of a genetic throwback, a coarse freckled face.

"Think so?" I say to him. "Think so?"

"Bet you," he says. His slitted eyes are muddy, antic.

I tell him with an oddsmaker's indifference that it's a bad bet, but he says no it's not, he can tell just by looking at me.

"Signor Risacca's been teaching you that skill?" I say. "Along with car repair?"

"Nope," the kid replies. "I do it on my own."

"Oh sure," I say, "me too, me too. It's not that we're suggestible or anything. We don't actually *like* the idea of having unnatural abilities, right?"

"Shit, I do!" the kid says. "I like it!"

I give him a big sour stare of derision but he doesn't get it—he's blind as a dog to facial expression. I think of him with all his barking, posturing friends, sniffing each other for their intentions. But he thinks he's gotten the upper hand; he wants to tell me his secrets now, mark me like a tree and then wander off with his nose to the ground.

"Show her *le candele*," the orange-haired kid says.

The girlish one, smirking, retrieves a Lavazza coffee can from the workbench behind him. He seems sure that I will try to snatch it from him; he holds the can in the crook of his arm, tips its rim towards me. The can is full of old spark plugs. I see cracked insulators, chewed-down gaps.

"This is what Signor Risacca teaches us," the dog-boy says. "We're learning about combustion."

"Not with those," I say. "Those are no good, are they?"

"Not for cars, no. But they're good for people."

The sun's levelling glare has erased the weeds and gutted Fiats in the yard outside, but to squint after them still feels like relief. I don't need this insinuating talk of combustion— not with the mayor burning up, not with the Masuccio's villa on fire.

"What's he telling you, 'for people'?" I say. "You need a fuel mixture to make those work, oxygen and something flammable—"

They have men's teeth in boys' faces, big scalloped incisors.

"We got fuel mixtures," the tall boy says. "Don't worry about that."

"Go on out back," says the other. "You'll see what we mean. Go ahead."

They think it's science; they think they've replicated their experiments and confirmed their findings, and now it's time to publish. It's hard not to like them like this, practicing the rudiments of enlightenment.

So I go back out into a day that's still like a long stare into a klieg light, just to get away from them. That's where Risacca finds me, in the remnants of an old olive grove behind the garage. I've waded through nettles and stiff grass; I've got tiny stinging cuts on my legs, chaff and dirt on my feet and a faint hammering behind my eyes. What I've found back there is disappointing, chilling—I've stepped back from it as if it were something putrid, something small and expected.

"Careful, *Professoressa*," Risacca says. "Watch your step." But even he sounds like it doesn't matter much.

It's the usual *opera*, a few common things transformed by odd usage into charms, motions and whispers made over them. Even as a kid I never thought I'd entirely bought the mumbo-jumbo, and faced with it now I feel only tired and repulsed.

Risacca and the boys have used those bad spark plugs like detonators; they've pushed pairs of them gap-down into the loose soil of a tiny groomed plot so that only their tops show. And between each set, like a stick of dynamite, is a plastic saint—one of those cheap souvenirs sold at grottoes and sanctuaries—buried to its neck. Their small elongated heads of yellow and blue look like something about to bloom.

"It's a faulty ignition module," Risacca says. "I don't have one in stock." Behind him a skeletal tabby prowls the garage foundation.

"Which of these was set for Signor Agretta?" I say.

He keeps his face still. "The one to the east," he says.

I look for it; it's no different from the others. A glow-in-the-dark plastic saint, greenish-white, like fungus.

"And Chiesa?" I say.

He recoils slightly. "Chiesa?"

"Is there one set for him?"

"What for?" he says. "He hasn't insulted me."

"He crossed you, though. You warned him not to, but he did."

Risacca turns from me a little, deflects my words; I'm saying things I'm not supposed to say. "That was his own people's law he broke, *Professoressa*, not mine," he says. "I'm just doing my job with him—law enforcement, like a cop. It's not personal."

There are olive branches just over our heads, twisted like ropes. I could pull myself up, I think, out of his sight.

"There was blood in the road to Alcamo this morning," I say. "That was someone doing their job, too, nothing personal. But it was still blood."

Risacca shrugs, watches the cat at its hunting. "What should I say?" he asks me. "It's all bloody at one time or another, everything we do. There's no way to tell."

154

"What's Agretta done to you?"

"No one does anything to me, *Professoressa*. They can try."

"It's for trying, then."

"I've put a few things in the ground. I haven't cut his throat."

"Because of his deal with Chiesa."

"As I said, he was free to try."

"But it was personal, him trying."

"It was, yes."

"That's for you to say? The mayor answers to you?"

"They all answer to me, *Professoressa*. All of my kind."

He pulls away from me slowly, like he's drawing a knife out of my ribs; the dead grass crackles under his feet. Those inquisitors in their red robes and clerical caps must have favored the same weighty, disjunctive stare he gives me now.

He has some nominal authority among the witches, then, vague prerogatives—he can move people up and down, bestow favors, issue directives, take powerful offense if he chooses. This is what they've all decided, without speaking, in their sleep. On the edge of my thoughts there's a fleshier, darker, harder Signor Masuccio with the same sort of grip on Alcamo, his villa not yet gone to seed.

"The car," I say, "what about the car?" and it's like someone speaking through my mouth, an effort that's not mine.

"The boys have switched a module out of another Lancia," Risacca says. "Take the car back to Chiesa, for God's sake. You've done enough for one day."

We've soured on each other as quickly as that. It's the car, I think—it's shown me to be a joyrider and him a voyeur of sorts, it's shunted us past civility. We've had enough of ourselves in the other's company.

Back in the garage the boys are chasing each other with a live soldering iron. Risacca tosses me the faulty ignition module; I catch it awkwardly against my sternum, a corner of it tapping my chest like it wants to get in.

"Chiesa will want the bad part," Risacca says. "Give it to him, will you?"

I heft the thing in my palm, consider throwing it at his head. But it's too cunning a bit of machinery to give up, a weighty little black box that might hold anything, jewels or a tendril of colored vapor—or computer chips with faces like satellite photos of cities, tiny grids of circuitry. It offers no hint of its purpose.

I know right then that I'm going to keep it. In return for that stolen gospel, I think. In return for Risacca's presumption.

On the drive back up to Valparuta a tour bus nearly sweeps me from the road, its great blunt whale's head swinging wide through a sharp curve. I yank the Lancia's wheel over, glimpse a depth of air, hanging vegetation in chimneys of rock; dust roils between us. In the shriek of the bus' brakes I hear the catastrophic end of that company's tours to Valparuta, German retirees on budget fares thrown against the seats in front of them, dentures and glasses broken, bruises and cuts, camera bags and bottled drinks falling from overhead bins.

Agretta's elaborate marketing scheme never had a chance. Valparuta was built to deflect invasion; it will keep its own secrets. I regain the narrow road, fishtailing, leave the aftermath of this near miss to others. I can feel that broken shock now, the car like a ship whose ballast has shifted.

CHAPTER EIGHTEEN

Nearly night now. The tall green salon doors to Chiesa's rooms stand ajar. He's surely heard me on the stairs but still I stop for a moment behind one narrow, opened-out panel, as if I've arrived with a speech rehearsed and wish to collect myself before I make my entrance. In fact I've come here mute, wordless; there's nothing in my head but a stuttering reel showing a tunnel's slaty dusk, a flood of unfelt sun. I'm the one with small offerings in my hands now, things snatched up to buy entry here and, this time, pardon. I've parked the dusty, ailing Lancia, leaking something now, in the tiny courtyard behind the hotel.

Centuries of paint clot the door's egg-and-dart carving; its knob is a great faceted pommel of red travertine.

Impatient, Chiesa clears his throat, ready to spit me out.

He's thrown his coat on the table, still wears the day's chert-gray Egyptian cotton and dark trousers. He's been waiting to go out on short notice—on word of my whereabouts, perhaps.

"I took your car," I say. "You left the keys in it."

He looks at me like I'm made of something cheap, a bad design. "Give them to me."

I toss him the keys, harder than necessary. He snatches them down in an overhand grab, puts them in a drawer. The back of his shirt is fiercely wrinkled.

I want to put down what I'm carrying, drop it all like an anchor and ride out Chiesa's anger on it, but he's blocking my path to the table.

"Was there a train?"

"Masuccio wouldn't hear of it. Bartolomeo drove me."

"All that way?"

"He insisted."

The table's open now, Chiesa after his cigarettes on the linen press. I let things fall from my hands, three links of hard dry cacciatore in knotted casings, a wedge of aged piave in pink paper. The woman at the salumeria had taken some dim shine to me, out too late and alone, got up in skirt and heels and shopping like a slut for a cold supper; she's given me an old prosecco bottle filled with surplus catarratto wine.

In the kitchen one fluorescent tube overhead flickers like an injured eye. I find two mismatched plates, a paring knife, two bar glasses; the tea towel has been replaced. I take too long in there, working at revising the meaning of that sooty, contained smoke I saw drifting from the back of the villa, folding and refolding the new tea towel until I can see Signor Masuccio clearly, his body smoldering like a burning mattress, already subsiding into the hard contours of the kitchen floor. He's hidden his face in his crooked arms; his hair falls in frizzles of grey ash on the shoulders of his scorched coat.

And Bartolomeo, having read his employer's eyes and understood the old man's obduracy as dispensation, has dropped Chiesa off and then taken himself to Trapani, driving the Masuccio family's aged, understated ride—a dark blue Bentley, maybe, its sides like a ship's hull. Bartolomeo will stay away from Alcamo for days.

The catarratto is too yellow, a color only good for blending, and tastes of cut grass. Chiesa takes up his glass and moves away again with a stoner's fluid automatism; he's high again, and he can see through walls, I think, he's that elevated.

"There was smoke from the Masuccio's house," I say. "No one answered at the gate."

He watches me butcher expensive cheese, chunks of it crumbling to bits, adhering to the knife's pot metal blade. "I had what I'd come for. I didn't want to wait," he says.

I feel my face go slack. "He gave it to you? The book?"

He takes a mouthful of wine, tastes it like food.

The knife falls from my hand, clatters on the plate. "You should report it, Chiesa. Masuccio needn't be implicated."

But all he does is return to the table to survey the food. He has that distant, determined look of one approaching a crowded buffet.

"I have a bad feeling about that smoke," I say.

Chiesa nods blandly, chewing; it may just be the cheese he's appreciating. "He released Bartolomeo from service, I think. Sending him off with me like that."

"Like a doomed man."

"Just like one, yes."

He's grazing the sausage now, tearing at the uneven little disks I've cut. He seems ready to consume anything set in his way.

The farmhouse chair behind the door is vacant, the trial records of the *benandanti* gone.

I ask him what he's done with the Cadmus.

He doesn't look up. "I've accessioned it into the collection," he says.

"You're joking."

"No."

159

"Under what provenance? How are you claiming to have come by it?"

Chiesa swallows, blots his lips on the back of his hand. "'Gift of an anonymous donor,'" he says.

I feel my guts, my joints go watery with laughter; it's too good, this claim of his, and utterly unassailable. Particularly if Masuccio is dead.

"He signed—?" I ask.

"Yes."

That briefcase Chiesa took from the back seat, carried into the house: clairvoyant or astute, he'd brought the proper forms with him.

"So the book disappears," I say. "Again."

He's back to sampling the ruined food. "It has a card in the catalogue," he says. "There's an accession record, a finding aid entry. It's here to be found, *Professoressa*; someone will find it."

In the course of this too-long day Chiesa's hair has gathered into heavy, oily strings; greying stubble shadows his jaws. He looks nothing like a force of nature—yet here he is, augmenting the archaeology of this book as if he were geologic time itself. There's something like genius in it.

"You've gone bonkers," I say.

"So you like it, too."

"It's good." There are artifacts, fossils, graves, caches, books and manuscripts layered in sediments and collections everywhere, waiting to be found; the Cadmus itself, I recall, first turned up among the relics of an exhumed saint. Chiesa has simply returned the book to its original state—buried, discoverable—and left it again to the laws of time and chance.

"You're not hungry?" Chiesa says.

I pick through the shards of cheese, but my mouth is dry. I resort to drinking the catarratto in gulps, just the thing for oiling a delinquent's confession.

"Your car didn't fare well today, Chiesa," I say. "It's really a piece of shit."

I watch pique and vague alarm come through the drug he's on like trees through fog.

"—The car?" he says.

It's all I can do not to squirm like a child. "They don't stand up to use, you know. Italian cars. Even Risacca says so."

"—Risacca?"

Whatever Chiesa's on it's good, it holds him down but lets him think. "You damaged the car," he says. "Risacca found you."

"A part failed, Chiesa—it wasn't me. You could have been driving."

He gives me a long, cool stare. "I have my old parts returned to me."

I tell him in a liar's steady voice then that Risacca has the part, that he wouldn't trust me to deliver it; I tell him that the car needs to go back to the shop anyway, he can get it then.

The module is downstairs, at the back of my armoire, pushed into the toe of a pair of unused walking shoes.

Chiesa holds an unlit cigarette just short of his lips. "The car must go back?"

"There's a broken shock or something."

It takes him a moment to be sure of what he thinks I've gone and done. But the drug steps in like expensive counsel, discreetly; instead of raising his voice he puts a hand to one stubbled cheek.

"You've wrecked my car," he says.

"It's a little banged up. I could wreck it for you."

He doesn't react. Sick with love, a cat in the hotel kitchen's trashbins cries like an infant.

Chiesa tilts his head to his lighter, snaps the flame. "You should have finished it off while it was yours, *Professoressa*."

"Joan," I say. "I'm Joan."

"This isn't how you do things, by halves. As if you weren't sure of yourself."

"You don't know how I do things."

He hugs his ribs as if the room were cold, cigarette held close to his face. "You wished to see Risacca, then? You damaged the car to summon him?"

"For God's sake, Chiesa—!"

"You see what will be made of it."

"I see what you're making of it."

He smokes without pause, every breath an acrid lungful. "That car is shit to me, *Professoressa*."

"You wanted me to wreck your car? You might have told me—!"

"You already knew."

"I—"

"You did. You know these things."

Like the bibliomane, he means—and the way I found the *benandanti* here with him, and the way I know this place. He's thrown them all in together, dreams, reason, memory— well, he told me they were all the same to him.

And then, bad timing: the wine arrives at my cerebral cortex, begins disassembling my thoughts. I laugh like someone caught out in a blunder.

"In Risacca's truck I thought maybe I had. Called him. On purpose." I'm swallowing my words back down as quickly as I say them. "Because it felt like I could take him on. But then I didn't. We got sick of each other, and I left."

"Sit down, *Professoressa*." He pulls a chair away from the table in a swift, screechy arc. He thinks I'm going to fall. But that's not my problem. My problem is my hair's on fire—a smoldering, latent blaze, like wires in a wall; that's why my head's so hot. I trail my fingers over the parlor's uneven plaster walls to Chiesa's bathroom, neglect to close the door. He has one of those cast-iron institutional sinks in there on thin tubular legs, a metal-framed mirror above it; there's an old bismuth-colored bathroom scale on the floor. I turn the cold tap on, put my head in the sink and feel my hair go heavy and inert, and a smell comes up from it like doused wood.

He's beside me then, fingers cradling my skull, cupping water over my scalp. He has the skill and warm disinterest of a hairdresser. He twists my hair into a rope, binds it in a thin hotel towel. I come up gasping, not so much reborn as shocked back to sensibility. But this feeling that I've been abruptly altered, that something has come over me, remains.

I must give him a shocky, guarded look; Chiesa retreats a little, keeps his hands where I can see them. "I have a sister," he says. "When she was married, they cut a meter and a half of hair from her head."

He had helped his sister wash her hair.

"Hair like yours?"

"No. She is *tizianesca*—auburn, like my mother."

Something cable-tight in me snaps. I sit down on the closed toilet, drag the towel from my head.

"Chiesa," I say, "I've seen his little no-man's land, out there behind the garage."

"It isn't pretty, is it?" He's put his hip against the sink, unbuttoned his damp cuffs.

"It isn't *anything*," I say. "It's dirt and plastic and junked auto parts."

He twists his wrists, rolls his cuffs. I think of all those tendons in his arms, the radius traversing the ulna: I could denounce the occult, elegant machinery of Chiesa's arm more easily than Risacca's little mess.

"That's not what we die of, you know," he says, and of course I do. I do know. It's what they believe that kills them.

The drain in the floor between us emits a subterranean gurgle, a whiff of methane. I scrub the towel over my head like a spent fighter.

"Tell me, Chiesa," I say. "How are you? I'm not going to raise your shirt this time."

He smiles faintly. "I'm well enough."

"No more—?"

"Infestations of my rooms? No."

"But you're high." I say it as if it's my failing, an inability to leave things unremarked.

He crosses his forearms, bare now and wood-colored, furred with black hair. "That's an entirely different set of demons," he says.

"You should just tell me that you like it, Chiesa, and I'd leave it alone."

But he doesn't.

Instead he pushes off from the sink and leaves the bathroom, returns with the catarratto and his cigarettes; he's lost his shoes, pulled his shirttail out, left our glasses on the table. He's got the bottle's neck in his fist. He lets himself slide down the sink's metal leg to the floor.

"And you, *Professoressa?*" He tips the bottle up, twists its mouth in his hand and passes it to me. "How are you?"

I take a good long pull. "There are two Masuccio sisters," I say. "One has hips, the other breasts."

"You saw them."

"I thought I did."

He nods; he knows this is an answer to his question.

In the corner behind me the ancient, calcined shower head spits, subsides; there's a rumbling of pipes in the walls. You never feel quite so human, quite so close to death as when you're in a bathroom.

"I don't know what I'm doing with these surveys anymore," I tell him.

It's a grave admission. I watch him absorb it—and then choose, deliberately, to misconstrue its meaning.

"Every researcher finds himself at sea in the middle of a project," he says. "It's the nature of the work."

"No—listen," I say. "I don't think I'm doing research anymore. I'm not sure I ever was."

He tips his head back against the sink's leg, closes his eyes. "Why tell me this, *Professoressa*? Do I look like an archivist to you?"

"I'm not talking to any archivist."

"Who, then?"

"The guy with the bloody nose. The one who devises journeys of instruction out into the countryside."

"The journey part—that wasn't me."

"Shut up, Chiesa. Yes it was."

He regards his curled fingers in his lap, lips twitching.

"Look," I say. "There's no Programme for Visiting Scholars anymore, is there? Not without Agretta."

He wants to hold his answer back, qualify it, but the lie's not in him. "No," he says. "That was his part of our bargain."

"And the Council wants you out."

"They do, yes. Are you going to keep that bottle all night, *Professoressa*?"

I swing the catarratto into his outstretched hand. It's left a taste of flowers in my mouth.

"What are we then, Chiesa?"

If we're not researcher and archivist—?

He shrugs, drinks. "Look at us, *Professoressa*." He gestures at the tiled, dingy walls, the seats we've chosen. "We are fallen, are we not?"

Somewhere in Valparuta's archaic sewer system a great charge of heated water caroms through a cistern; a smell of petrochemicals and nitric acid rises from the floor.

A laugh of sorts escapes me, grades into a cough. "A fallen archivist, then," I say. "A fallen scholar."

Chiesa shrugs again, eyes me over the bottle: why not?

It's Chiesa's doing, then, his native impulse to perseverate, that lets us go on as we were but changes our state, throws us forward.

We sit just as we are for a while, the bottle passing between us; I think we feel the lightness, the vacuum of purpose that vagrants enjoy. We talk in fits and starts, Chiesa stubbing cigarettes out on the tile floor. I pull my fingers through my matted, drying hair, thinking that I must look a little used like this, a little past my prime.

I tell him very little. Nothing of the ruin I've made of my career, nothing of my ties to Sicily—yet I seem to say too much. I fall into listing for him the collections I've plumbed, choice items from the vast inventory of lost things I've catalogued: a stable full of blooded Turkish horses, all named for Muslim prophets; a jewelled skull engraved with clan tattoos; gilded predellas, bolts of green silk, a silver monstrance set with rubies.

Chiesa wears the respectful, waiting face of a veteran physician; he already knows what ails me but lets me finish my dull reportage anyway.

"You'd have all those lost things back," he says. "A perverse nostalgia."

I stagger to my feet then, let the towel fall to the floor. I have to step over his legs to reach the door and as I do he holds the bottle up to me, negligently, as if I were a passing waitress. "You choose it over mourning, this impossible task of yours," he says. "Why not just learn to mourn? Take it," he says, and lays the bottle's neck against my hip.

The last swallow of the catarratto is warm and tastes of spittle. Chiesa's fingers close around my ankle.

I let the bottle fall from my hand, shatter on the floor. Wicked little scimitars of greenish glass scatter over the tiles.

Chiesa glares up at me, grinning with fury and disbelief. For weeks to come we'll only find the tiniest shards with the soles of our feet.

I take his shirtfront in both fists then and haul him up, grapple with him; he lays hold of the silk knotted at my waist and I push his hands down, make him put a hand up my skirt. His body is hard, concave; his clothing foils me, maddens me. I find his mouth with mine.

These silent, complex agreements that people can reach— to cease what's futile, to acknowledge what's unspoken and let it stand. We have whole embassies in our heads that are utterly dark to us, that negotiate in the spaces between our words and gestures and return us pacts we never knew we signed.

And so he comes to me in his disordered bed, his skin lit grey by an incomplete dark. He's so thin, he's thin as Christ, and drifts of fading bruises run the length of his body, marking him all the way down his thighs. Yet he seems to feel no pain. Only once, somewhere in our ensuing mutual struggle to satisfy and be satisfied, does he cry out hoarsely, as if I've cut him.

CHAPTER NINETEEN

My mother wore her hair like an unmarried girl's all her life, long and with a fringe of bangs that friends could trim for her. She would shake it impatiently away from her face, push it off her forehead with her palm; it was her pride, a flag she carried. Men shouted vulgarities at her in the street because of it. She shouted back, slogans from the women's movement, the anti-Mafia movement, the human rights movement. Men never turned back to bully her quiet; they knew she was crazy. My mother didn't care why they finally let her be. It was a victory either way. She shook her hair like a horse's mane and made sure there were witnesses.

Every moment with my mother was like this. Everything she did and said, where she lived, who her friends were, the things she ate, wore, bought, read—it was all declamatory, all argument. In a country where the reasons for things were entirely clandestine, among people whose very deviousness carried an air of resignation, my mother declared her convictions, defined herself by them. She stood out; her beliefs were unshakable.

In this way, she hid herself entirely. I never knew her. Maybe Russell did, imperfectly, for a short time. But somehow I think that even her liaison with Russell was ultimately a gesture, myself a powerful symbol to her of her own striving. Like the way she wore her hair, my mother carried me to provoke outrage. The difference was that she let me go. She never relinquished anything else.

We inhabit the library like sleepwalkers now, Chiesa and I, moving through the stacks on unresolvable missions, bending sightless, staring, over books and texts. Chiesa has begun repairing all the volumes—all of them, he says— whose covers have come loose. I hear him at a distance coughing, shifting books on shelves; one hits the floor with the sound of a door slamming. He carries great corkscrewed stacks of damaged books to the circulation desk and labors indiscriminately over them, lifting torn endpapers, mending broken joints, consolidating the fraying corners of worthless buckram bindings. He'll never live long enough to finish the task he's set himself.

"Come down," he says as I pass him on some obscure errand of my own. "Come down from there." His speech is thick, garbled, not his own; it's not me he's seeing.

As for myself, I leave my desk in the archives again and again—standing and listening for sounds I either hear or expect to hear, the shriek of the chair I've pushed back still in my ears. I have an antenna's lean and quiver then, and I'm sure I hear the faint alarms that send me into the stacks as if they were on fire, or sinking, or shaking themselves to pieces. I go in like a rescuer but I don't know what to save, there's too much; composure leaves me. I shove Hollinger boxes under my arm, pull down armfuls of books and carry them out, gimping under the load I've taken. And I think I hear the demise of what I leave behind, too, its undetermined but certain end in a roar that sounds like turbines, like a plunge into water. Some worried part of me is tapping on the glass through all of this, mouthing the words *madness, madness,* but all I do is drop my salvage on the desk and try to read it all.

It's voodoo we've resorted to, making the empty, obsessive motions of what has slipped away from us in the hope of calling it back: Chiesa's job, the purpose of my work. We exercise ourselves this way to no effect, and thank God for that—there's no telling what we'd even do if by some unnatural chance those things came back to us reanimated. They'd seem monstrous to us now, untenable—and silent as ever on where we might go from there. This vacuum that we fill with old gestures saves us.

We take each other indiscriminately now too, wherever we find ourselves: in a smear of creased papers on Chiesa's desk, on the floor of the archives. Once on the stairs to his rooms at the hotel Chiesa presses me against the wall and does me there, like a date fuck, my thighs slung in his hands. It's all reflexive, wordless, punctuated by sounds of effort like sobs. We rock like the bereaved, like neglected children.

For days at the end of that last summer we had water only sporadically in my mother's stifling flat. We carried water that we could not drink from the public fountain three streets over, filling cast-off plastic Fanta bottles, saucepans and buckets at its splattering faucet, enduring the silent scrutiny of people there who didn't know us. My mother spoke like a teacher in front of a class as we staggered back home with our bottles and pans. *Nearly half our water leaks out of broken pipes before it gets to our houses,* she said. She looked at me but spoke to everyone else. *And then what's left is diverted*

*to those who've paid off the water commissioner. They want to water
their gardens, you know. They want to wash their cars.*
I knew she was instructing others. I walked with my
head down, my face and hands still cool from the fountain and my hair dirty—invisible, negligible—yet wronged
by corrupt public figures, too, entitled to an outrage that I
couldn't capture. I felt made of glass, as if comprehension
passed through me like light. *We must take our complaint before
the City Council,* my mother told me. But I knew that I would
never go there with her.

Russell was in the *soggiorno* when we returned, studying
the room's spoiled Baroque frescoes. The summer's excavations had ended; he had been working at Busoné on the
island's opposite coast, and had not come to Palermo all
summer.

For five days my parents' bed smelled like a plowed field,
and they smelled of each other—water was too precious to
pour over such fundamental odors. My parents forced a year
of cohabitation into a single American work week; in the evenings the flat was full of my mother's friends, passionate talk
and cigarette smoke. Russell took everything but my mother
as artifact, tolerating the parties and the rabble of visitors,
making polite conversation, but he didn't like what he saw.

My mother's darkroom was just off the *soggiorno*, in a
china closet she had had gutted and plumbed. She kept her
print file in four metal filing cabinets in the big shabby living
room, pushed up against walls the color of overripe fruit.
Photographs of Mafia killings were scattered over the work-
table there, dead men in rooms, alleys and automobiles, black
lakes of blood.

She was called out with her camera at all hours that
summer. She knew people everywhere; the police would
arrive to find her already there, shooting rolls of film.

On the fourth night of that week Russell followed her out of the bedroom as she snatched up keys, camera, handbag. He was naked under cut-off sweatpants, still fumbling with the drawstring. Something had occurred to him.

"What have you been doing with Giovanna when this happens?"

Me. Giovanna.

I watched from a cot in the *soggiorno*, where I slept with my mother's work. The bodies didn't frighten me. They were like abandoned *palazzi*, ruined and empty, their windows broken out. Palermo was full of them.

My mother shrugged, lit a cigarette, kept moving. "Well, *caro*, what do you think?"

She let him think that she had left me alone in her crumbling apartment while she photographed bodies. The next morning the telephone rang; a man's filtered voice told Russell that Simona Origo's photographs would burn.

She knew she would never see me again. On that last day she took a photograph of me standing before tall salon doors that opened onto nothing; the doorway had been bricked up. I have a suitcase at my feet. Already I have the look of someone too sure of all outcomes. This was the photograph she sent me that fall, at Russell's place in Providence, instead of a picture of herself.

But my mother hadn't left me alone in the apartment that summer. She had taken me with her.

I think I hear the squeal and boom of torqued sheet metal, the stacks tipping, tipping, ready to fall like old trees do on a still day when their time has come. I go in there in a panic and books fall into my arms, marking my skin with their weight. There's a mountain of books and papers on my desk, heaps of them on the floor. I hold each page of text to my face so that it fills my vision—a monument, a monument—and commit what's there to memory: tables of contents, indices, fawning dedications; technical pamphlets, old train schedules, novels, letters bearing long-expired news.

She'd rouse me up at night, my mother, push shoes on my bare feet, wrap me in a coat despite the hot darkness. She was robbing the apartment of me, a clandestine removal; she was padding me against the bumps and swerves of illicit transport. Her hands drew me along in the dark—a light in our window, she whispered, would send the men standing like statues in the street below gliding away to make phone calls. It was a kind of cruel game, her hushed, pressured speech told me, one she was good at and enjoyed. She played it without compunction among the innocent, like a high speed chase.

We'd leave by way of a sunken service door, wriggling between the bent bars of its grate and hauling ourselves up into a side alley too narrow for cars. And then she would press me into her side and we'd run—clumsily, stumbling, hindering each other—to the all night clinic a few streets down, where a taxi could always be found, its engine idling. There were addicts like bundles of old clothes in the clinic's waiting room chairs, a prostitute holding her beaten face. It seemed a giant hand had set them out there in the clinic's plate glass window; no one would choose to sit in such an awkward, exposed place.

Simona would misdirect the driver, send him past the crime scene, robbing him of a later opportunity to lie elaborately to the police. We left bills on the seat and the car doors standing open to delay him following us.

Those black, breathless travels back, to come knowingly upon the dead—as if we'd planted them there ourselves—reside in me now. I may be made entirely of those journeys. My willful mother held me before her, against her body, whispering raggedly into my hair *It's nothing, it's nothing, you're not afraid, are you? Brave girl!* I'd go stiff in her arms, outraged; I'd seen her show the same unseemly ardor to Russell when she wanted her way, putting her mouth to his as if to drink from him. She caressed me fiercely, moved me forward. I was the air she displaced on her way to the dead, an incline she took without breaking stride. She told me they were nothing, those leaking bodies thrown into corners and doorways, but they were everything to her. I was the one she could discount.

And she couldn't see it, how she'd deluded herself: those violent, commonplace deaths she met like lovers really were nothing—she couldn't make them into instruments of change, not with a camera or anything else. She rushed unseeing through the standing proof of this night after night, all those decaying buildings wearing their plumbing on their walls like inscriptions. Everything would stay the same; the city had been built of something immutable. Those nighttime journeys, the screams and entreaties of the freshly bereaved, the dry silence of my mother's flash, empty as heat lightning—nothing came of them. I learned from them how blood smells, poured out in volumes onto pavement and upholstery, a smell of impending rain. I learned to watch, repeatedly, the spectacle of my own abandonment.

Too late, I've come to understand that I'm made of this, of Palermo's enduring darkness, the certainty of nothing.

CHAPTER TWENTY

Sabrina Agretta visits me in my rooms.

I know Chiesa's knock by now and this one's not his, though it's come so late in the evening that it could not properly be another's. It's the hour for assignations, venal husbands travelling to their mistresses' doors under cover of the restaurants closing, a final population of the streets.

I don't move from my chair. I've thrown a towel over its sticky brocade and occupied it in my underwear, a bad monograph on the Venetian silk trade open on my knees. If it were Chiesa knocking I'd wrap myself in the towel and let him in without a word, but now I keep very still, the blood singing like insects in my ears.

She speaks through the door. "*Professoressa*," she says. "Let me in."

I hate her peremptoriness, her knowledge that I'm here. I get up only after I've thought of several ill-bred responses and settled instead for silence: if she knows so much, why answer her?

In the bedroom I throw on a dark crepe de chine shift and push my bare feet into heels to meet her. We've had one companionable encounter and I've seen her show an iron self-possession—I should like her but I don't, I don't, because the mayor's striking wife, with her uncut hair and improper concern for Chiesa, is the one who's somehow gutted him; she was his fiancée.

At the door she looks me up and down, annoyed and interested. Her fingers don't quite touch my hair, my dress. "This is how it's done?" she says. She might try it, her tone suggests, if this really is *la moda americana*.

She follows me into the room and takes the chair I offer her. Her linen dress is creased across the lap from a long day's wear, but if she's fatigued or worried I don't see it. She arranges her hair with a few practiced movements, discreetly appraises my rooms.

"You can live with so little of your own?" she says. "So vagabond?"

"It doesn't bother me," I say.

She grants this with a little moue; there's no accounting for others' tastes. "You're comfortable here with us, then," she says.

I won't allow it. I tell her that I can live anywhere.

"Ah," she says appreciatively, as if I've told a mild joke.

There's a towel on the floor, a blouse drying on a hanger in the window. I've shoved my largest suitcase behind the desk, where it still violates the room like a goat byred in a house. The place must look half-claimed to her, cluttered with the indifferent business of mere occupancy; no one seems resident here.

"My work requires it, Signora Agretta," I say.

She finds this even more preposterous; I watch her quell her reaction like a sneeze. She composes herself, adjusts her measure of me downward. "Please, you must call me Sabrina, after admitting me to your rooms so late and unannounced," she says, and flashes a dimpled smile. She runs this girlish charm out like a cannon when she needs it, to breach opponents' walls.

"If you'd been a mere Sabrina, Signora Agretta, I wouldn't have let you in," I tell her. "Perhaps it's best that both of us remember who you are."

Her smile narrows, sharpens. "Perhaps it is, then," she says pleasantly. She scans the floor around her, as if she's dropped something. "Signor Chiesa is well, I trust?" she says.

"Climb two more flights of stairs, Signora, and you can ask him that yourself."

"I don't ask you this to save myself the climb, *Professoressa*."

Or to save her reputation—if she cared what others thought of her she would have cut her hair.

She stretches upright in her chair, a tiny, prideful movement. "You were not yet friends, you and Signor Chiesa, when we last spoke," she says. "I think you know him now."

I feel my face flush. "You know him, too," I say.

She struggles a little with this; she's not a prevaricator. "I knew him once," she says.

"You have a history with Chiesa."

"All wives have such histories," she says. "But I am respectably married—no one can say otherwise."

"He dreams of your tongue, Signora Agretta—of boxing it like a velvet ribbon. Chiesa is less philosophical than you."

She curls the fingers of one hand against her sternum, leans in over them. "Is it my fault?" she cries. "Am I to blame for his paralysis of mind? I'll tell you, *Professoressa*: he and I were *fidanzato*, engaged for many years. But he waited too long; I broke it off."

"To marry Agretta."

Her shrug is magnificent. "And so?" she says.

"You knew they were rivals."

I'm no more annoyance to her than a crooked hem.

"You don't know anything," she says. "I waited! What, was I to make a vocation of it? I was teaching the children of my friends, *Professoressa*—of those I'd gone to school with myself. He'd left me—"

"He was *working*."

"Working, yes!" She sweeps an errant silver bangle from her forearm to her wrist. "Other women lose their men to wars. We lose ours to mainland jobs."

"He told you he was coming back."

She won't even waste a gesture, a disarrangement of her limbs for this. "They all think they're coming back, *Professoressa*," she says. "Or else they'd never leave."

Something minor, silly, contracts in me—a small pain. She sees it, my gaze slanting off into uncertainty. Everyone concedes this round to her, I think; that or her cause seems so self-evident to her that she never feels imperiled, never takes offense.

"A girl must make a good match for herself, *Professoressa*," she says. "The heart can catch up later."

Outside a distant, isolated gunshot reverberates like a stone dropped down a well.

She nods toward the open window. "A celebration," she says.

I hear it now too, the faint static of laughter, cut off by the close of a door—the shooter returning to the party.

There's silence from Chiesa's rooms above us.

"There's something you must do for me," Sabrina Agretta says.

It isn't much. I'm to relay an invitation to the archivist to visit her at home.

"Ask him to come on Thursday," she says. "Ask him to bring his bathroom scale."

I study her for a moment, this maverick, unconventional woman. She rests her ornamented hands demurely in her lap; her good looks lie at the ready, like knives in an open drawer.

"No," I say.

"But whyever not?"

"These are cures for ignoramuses and hysterics, Signora."

She flushes furiously; I wasn't to know. "How did you—" she begins but then craft intervenes again; she turns sullen. "He's told you."

"He hasn't."

"How, then?"

"I have my own fund of knowledge."

Her eyes widen. "For this? What do you know?"

"I've seen it before. Household objects appropriated in the exercise of magic."

"Exercise!" she cries. "Must it be exercised, then? Like a restive horse?"

I think of Risacca's modest construction under ragged olive trees, Chiesa's self-contempt. "It seems that it must," I say.

"Then you will talk to him."

"No." I see Chiesa on the hotel stairs, shouldering that old bismuth-colored scale as if it were a weapon. He will hate himself for it.

"It's his *dovere, Professoressa*—it is his duty. He must come."

"Then he hardly needs my urging, does he? Chiesa's nothing if not punctilious."

The room's lights go brown, then flare unnaturally; a filament blows in one of my bedroom lamps.

She's twisting the bracelet on her wrist as if it were a manacle. There'd be silence if not for the air's continued radio crackle. "He does not like the work," she says. "He feels that it shames him."

I'm to coax Chiesa along then, take him playfully by the necktie and lead him shambling, grinning, past his aversion.

The room turns the color of pond water again. I get up, gasping; if I were to do what she's asking of me I would breathe like this, as if from a diminishing pocket of trapped air.

"He must do it either way," she tells me. "It will do no harm to ease his feelings on this." She waits for me to understand, but I'm still trying to find the remnants of the room's breathable air. I start and stop around the room like a suffocating fish.

I see it on her face then: it's my fault if fate overhears her now. "His state of mind is not good, *Professoressa*," she says. "You know it's not."

That distant celebration spills into the night again, rearmed and giddy; multiple shots are fired off, the long flat crack of rifles, a shotgun's deep cough. I know how these things go, the men pushing through terrazzo doors in their limp synthetic finery, gaudy narrow shirts they bought when they were bachelors, the buttons straining now. Those are their grandfathers' old field guns they clasp across their chests and fire into the air from their hips like guerillas. They look like farm implements, those old guns, lengths of pocked iron in scarred wood fittings. They could be shovels, hoes. The men keep the lit room at their backs and peer out into the dark, laughing, shouting. No one looks too long at the night or the few shapes that swim out from it: a shed's corrugated roof, a parked car's glinting insect bulk. They fire into the dark as if to kill it.

Bored and jealous, their wives watch from low yellow couches inside.

I wish I were there, scratching that party's hard veneer.

Upstairs Chiesa lies on his face like a toppled statue, unmade bedsheets twisted beneath him. His eyes move as if they're following lines of text.

"There are others who do good works," I say. "Let him be."

"Don't you think I would?" She looks into the room's dim corners, on guard for what might overhear us. "I don't want to trouble him. He's like a lost boy, he'd walk in front of trains—"

"Leave him alone, then!"

"No—he must do it."

The gunfire has set the dogs chained out under rabbit hutches and chicken coops barking; the night erupts like an over-full kennel. I hear the ring of chains yanked tight, bodies against fences. By the time the noise subsides the men are gone, they've fled what they've touched off, like pranksters.

"He's been placed above the others, *Professoressa*," Sabrina Agretta slips into the fading racket.

She waits for the significance of her words to arrive upon me, waits impatiently as if it were a tardy guest. Its failure to appear becomes an inexcusable affront; as a few still-crazed dogs yip and bellow in the dark I watch her lose her temper, all her smooth deep mannerisms curling away. Provoked past decorum she speaks quickly, her eyes on the ceiling. She thinks what she is forced to say is stupid, or so she'd have me believe; she wants me to think well of her.

"They say the drum that summons them is his," she says.

Her tethered, ferocious little smile says that she will never forgive me for forcing her to speak these words—never.

Chapter Twenty-One

Chiesa shows up at my door with that old scale like a stone in his hands, something he's cleared from a field. As we talk he hefts it awkwardly from side to side, from shoulder to hip, his arms tiring. The scale's ornate needle quivers over hand-painted numbers. I won't let him in with it.

"Come with me," he says.

I lean in the doorway, blocking his entry with a hand on the jamb. "You sound like you're used to seeing that work."

"Seeing what work?"

"'Come with me.'" I stir as if I'm curious, but I don't move my arm. "What is that on a drum, 'come with me'? A beat to arms? A mustering tattoo?"

He won't watch me behave like this, stares off down the hall.

"Try a drum," I say. "I'm staying here."

"You should come."

"I wouldn't presume. It's for you to do."

"Some anthropologist."

My lungs fill with something unbreathable. "You want a notetaker there? Someone with a microphone? You should see yourself, Chiesa."

"I do see."

"What are you going to do? Put it in the trunk of your car and drive it over there like it's equipment? Like you need it to conduct a procedure?"

"It's how it's done."

"For God's sake, Chiesa—"

He swings the scale up between us. "It's not for me," he says. "Agretta needs the scale."

"And it's you who must weigh him."

He closes his eyes. "Yes."

"You're just another crappy charm for them to pin their hopes on, Chiesa. You know? It's how they see you, a broken thing that's been repurposed."

"They're not stupid."

I have to admit they're not, looking at him. The scale's weight drags his shoulder down, pulls tight the cords in his neck. He's down to sinew-wrapped bone and a dry clear heat that comes off him like light; he bruises me now when he puts his weight on me.

He's dressed in American sportswear for Sabrina Agretta's eyes, to camouflage his illness. The bright polo shirt and khakis invite her to discount him—he wants to seem just another male in bright plumage to her, vain and given to promiscuity. Maybe he feels fortunate that he hasn't been discarded outright. Maybe he feels that he owes it to her to make this easy.

"This isn't even going to cost her, is it?" I say.

"Of course it is," he says. "I charge a fee."

I shut the door in his face.

And then I try to muffle the vacant day, stuff it with a long twisted cloth of useless activity like a bell that needs silencing.

I rush down to the library in the rising heat, take the locked front doors in my hands and shake them the way Risacca did, with steady force, not for entry but just to task them for being locked against me. I try to force a side door, a window; I stop short of breaking glass, a scruple that seems ridiculous to me given what's at stake. No one speaks to me or tries to turn me aside—we all know where Chiesa's gone.

I give up on the library, hurry back to the Elimo as if I'm on a string. Grey tissues of dried milk and tarry rinds of oil and wine still adhere to the streets, unremarked now; the *Valparuti* park their cars on them, stab the kickstands of their *motorini* into them. They're indistinguishable from the effects of something real, an overturned grocery truck or the overflow of a dumpster long since moved. In time everyone will say they saw that rush of rancorous spirits through the streets; they'll point out the stained cobbles, repeat the stories of those who claimed to have whirled along in the spirits' wake, and then there'll be no room for doubt.

Chiesa has gone to weigh the mayor for God's reckoning.

It's an old impulse among farmers, the anxious tallying and retallying of harvests as the time to take them in nears—as if those numbers written, repeated, considered, amended might hold off an ill-timed rain, deter cutworms like prayer. They'll appeal to anything, anything at all for help.

Agretta, too, is ready to fall from the vine. And so he'll be weighed, and weighed again and then once again, in hope that the witches won't dare cheat God further of His harvest, the steady fall of chosen souls before His blade.

Like Church iconography, there's only formal beauty to admire in this kind of thought. The rest is cant to me, delusion.

The narrow salon doors to Chiesa's flat are bolted, too. I put my back against them, their carvings like another bony spine against my own as I slide down to the floor. I've given up too easily. There are odd little *botteghe* on shadowed side streets selling red leather handbags, Turkish brass, old mourning jewelry, shoes beautiful as sculpture—I could have pretended to shop for an hour or two, made a private game of extricating myself from salesgirls' genteel coils. I could have occupied myself through Agretta's weighing. But I fall to the floor in this neglected corridor instead, I let gravity carry me down. The stuttering images that come to me are welcome and regrettable as sleep.

This is what I think I see:

Chiesa, shouldering the scale, forms a procession of one, crosses a lake of tiled floor. Sabrina watches from a doorway, folded arms barricading her heart. Outside, the garden has just been watered; disturbed wasps hover over the wet beds. The house is modern, expansive, its parlors set with groups of slim-legged chairs and sofas holding conversations of their own.

There's a flood of useless sunlight in the sickroom, a crowd of potted hibiscus against the glass. The room's yellow walls move like curtains. Black antique furniture—a huge bombe chest of drawers, a lacquered armoire, a blemished cheval mirror, three ball-and-claw side chairs and an ornate toilet chair—stands massed against one wall: the heirloom boudoir set passed for generations to the eldest, like a curse. There's a monstrous, finialed bed marooned in the middle of the floor.

I distrust it entirely, this florid, super-real vision of mine. It can't be the scene at Agretta's house—the bed is empty. The flowers' coarse, fleshy blooms have gone brown at their edges; Chiesa has sweated through his colorful shirt. Sabrina tugs a loose thread at the neck of her blouse and feels a seam give. But I can't fill the bed, can't locate Agretta in this tableau, and so the whole thing falls.

The hallway floor is gritty with dust. My hands come away from it soiled, stuck with tiny stones. Below me a guest vacates his room, slams the door as if to end an argument.

Chiesa will tell me if I ask that yes, there was a chest of drawers there whose sides and elaborately inlaid front swelled like something about to burst. He'll confirm the presence in the room of flowering plants in need of some attention. It should mean nothing to anyone. These things are found in every home of means where illness has intruded. And who knows better than I how distant rooms are furnished— how distress alters their surfaces, draws people in and out of their doors?

I gather myself up, climb to my feet. Midday light has flooded the dirty corridor.

I make my way back down the stairs to overbright fixtures, numbered doors opening onto a runnered hallway marked by a carpet sweeper.

I let go of my tainted, substandard imaginings; I wish for de Quincey's unreasonable visions.

CHAPTER TWENTY-TWO

Detached from earth, in this fortress town of air and stone where sight is curtailed by walls, I've come to think that August's long siege of dust and sunlight will never end. The days' volatile hours have all burned off; what's left is a glassy, irreducible slag of time that repeats itself endlessly, that must be met every morning and somehow traversed. Nights are no better—nothing but the burned days' banked coals, stifling and firebox black. Chiesa is a doctor, a priest, a mercenary whose services have been retained, and he will say little now about his client or his obligations to her. I've blown my chance to know what words he'll speak, what gestures he'll make in Agretta's sickroom, the tenor of his strained exchanges with Sabrina. I'll not be taken into confidence now.

I ask him: "You'll go again next week? And the week after that?"

Chiesa closes his shirt collar, cinches up his tie. We've fallen together again in a narrow canyon of books at the library's limits, its cramped dimness both incitement and cover to our iniquity.

"My fee's been paid in advance," he says. "Are you going to get up?" He works his belt with absent efficiency, three clean motions of his hands.

But I think I might lie here for a while, a single extinction awaiting slow burial. My skirt is still pushed up; I've left palm prints on the floor.

No doubt she's paid him in cash—one of those anomalous transactions no one wishes to declare. I stir there on the old marble floor, gather my legs under me. Chiesa knows better than to offer me a hand.

"I'll catch up with you," I tell him, "go ahead." I don't want him to see me stagger to my feet like someone who's been knocked to the ground.

"Don't fail to find me," he says. "You must witness and countersign the storage room inventory."

I look up at him as if he were a puzzling sky, empty of cause for a sudden shift in the weather.

"Michaelmas is coming, you know," he says. "There'll be an accounting." He runs a hand over his hair, tugs his shirt-front straight.

I can't even find a string of words long enough, tensile enough to slow his leaving.

And so I grope after what I let fall from me in those first indecorous moments with Chiesa: pen and a scrap of paper, my shoes, an earring that had caught in clothing. It's a shameful little harvest that I undertake on hands and knees, on marble the color of salt pans—a kind of scrabbling for shards after I've deliberately broken myself.

I'll not be mended this time. My fingers fumble up an old dust-furred coin from under the stacks, lost years ago and never missed.

Michaelmas is coming.

Chiesa's in a dingy back room, bent over a clipboard of curled pages. He sips a breath between his teeth, lifts my collar from my sweating neck.

"You shouldn't hurry in this heat."

"I've lost track of time, Chiesa."

He checks his watch. "This won't take long. Come, just sign." He turns the clipboard in his hands; I stop it.

"It's not still August?"

"Of course not, *Professoressa*. We're a week into September."

There's broken equipment on steel storage shelves in here, depleted supplies of paper goods.

"But the August holidays—" I say.

"*Ferragosto?* You didn't feel the town empty out?"

I hadn't. It had been there to feel, not see—and so I'd missed it.

"Chiesa," I say. "They're going to fire you at Michaelmas."

He lifts a dusty old reel-to-reel, fouled in its own power cord, and searches its heavy, complicated body for a serial number. I hook my fingers on the edge of a shelf and lean there, breathing as if I've climbed.

How careless, how clever of me to inhabit Valparuta as if it were only an altered state and not a place at all. And how dark of Chiesa to show me only his failing, addicted self, seemingly motionless in these long flashes of light that have passed for days. We've known all along, really, that the venal, chicken-hearted Council would slip his firing into the grave business of Michaelmas—the annual, obligatory settling of rents and accounts, when St. Michael Archangel sits in fierce judgment of mortal affairs.

We've been drinking each other like laudanum.

I want to ask him what we're going to do, but I know the eyes he'll turn on me.

So we'll take the car, maybe, drive until the money runs out. We'll pass ourselves off as researchers in the libraries of the larger resort towns—where the sun makes idiots of people—and steal their valuable books to pay for meals and ill-furnished rooms, car repairs, cigarettes, alcohol. It won't last long.

Something comes loose in me and I go buoyant, rudderless; I've been grifting like this for years, using up my chances, burning people like matches. I knew it would end sometime, and badly, but this feeling of sudden latitude takes me by storm. I can do anything now, anything to preserve the two of us.

I sign Chiesa's inventory. The brittle paper tears under the pen; I hand the clipboard back to him, and while his hands are full and he can't fend me off I cup his testicles in my hand, through the drape of trouser fabric. My grin is that of a habitual offender.

The Reference desk is deep in Chiesa's restoration projects—backless books, texts flayed out of their covers. I hardly see them. Those rescue operations I've been running into the archives serve me now like drills, only this time I know what to take. I lay my hands on the card catalogue's handsome old face and start to work. It doesn't take me long. The white edges of a new card announce the Cadmus's entry in advance of my walking fingers.

I take the Cadmus Gospel, still in its phase box. Chiesa has made a neat job of it. I'd say I remember him measuring and cutting the box's soft card, setting its creases with a straightedge and bonefolder, but he did it in secret, out of my sight.

He's never asked me to check my bags at the desk. The little boxed book fits down into the satchel I carry in and out every day. On my way out of the archives I duck into the stacks once more, take the de Quincey too.

This one I don't even bother to hide. I carry it out of the library in my upturned hand, like a paperback, its spine in my palm.

And once outside I see it for the first time: the sun's force has waned fractionally, it stands a little lower in a newly-colored sky. Valparuta is walled like a cemetery but that doesn't matter, the declining season works like the pull of tides, drawing all things toward it. If I consult my corrupted memory of light like this I know what I can't see from here: grapevines torn and drooping in the harvesters' wake, the shuddering processions of laden tractors stalled at the gates of the *cantine sociali*. The *vendemmia*, the grape harvest, has begun.

Michaelmas, I recall, has its own Ember Days. The night battles will be fought again soon, in the wake of the *vendemmia*.

CHAPTER TWENTY-THREE

There's no getaway bag packed and stowed under my bed, no thick rubberbanded roll of blue bills waiting at the back of a drawer to fund escape. But I watch the suddenly active sky and street with an inventory in my head of what will go with me when it's time: jewelry and my most provocative pair of heels; that silk wrap and a revealing blouse to assist in our con of covetous librarians; a zippered fleece; a pair of jeans; those unused walking shoes for the desperate end of our run.

The Cadmus. The de Quincey. My passport and bankbook.

The faulty ignition module; it's mine like a sin committed.

And the handled canvas bag I'll carry it all out in, something a vain woman would carry for a long day at the beach. No one will know that I'm leaving for good.

But I don't leave. There's a hard, monitory part of me that advises getting out now, before Chiesa is repudiated and embarrassment attaches itself to us, before the night battles make him ever more sick of himself. The dry lakes of days wait for me to persuade him of this. They give me all the time I might need to wear him down with arguments and pleading; they provide an unobstructed view of the monotonous, finite days ahead. We're alone in arid companionable silence for hours—I might convince him if I tried. But our next career will be our last. I can't bring myself to take it up quite yet.

The ground gives way beneath our feet: already, the night battles' prodromal vandalism and chicanery has begun. Pilfered fruit, stolen license plates, locks drilled out of security gates lie abandoned in the street; six trussed and seasoned chickens sit on the curb like ruffians. Anomalous smears of blood and dirt appear on walls—from where? from where?—and an entire dinner service is laid out on the rim of a dumpster, as if awaiting a party of jackals.

Chiesa yaws away from these provocative assemblages but he's not repelled, he's afraid to get too close. I trail him on the street now, hanging back for the view of him but critical of his stooping gait, his appalling thinness. He works to breathe, grimacing; he works to climb the streets. I won't be seen with him like this and yet he's worthy of protection, like any ruined statesman. I imagine stepping between him and his assailants.

Walk up! Walk up! he cries, and falls against a wall to wait for me. A thin rain of tiny calcified seashells ticks off his shoulders; his voice is high and faint. I shake my head, wave him on but when I reach him he's still breathless, still has a hand on the wall. He won't meet my eyes. He would have gone on ahead if he could have, just to spite me. He knows how close I really want him.

"Why do you lag behind?" he wheezes. "Are you not my colleague?"

I am—and I am not. I shade my eyes while he stoops and breathes.

"Michaelmas falls on the Thursday this year," I say. "You'll go out at night—you and the others you lead—on the feast of the Archangel."

He raises a palm to me. "Not now," he says.

My gaze falters as if he's injured me, as if I am bewildered. The view down the street is precipitous, the houses falling away, the hill like a rising tide. There are those fossil shells under Chiesa's hand—the floor of an old, shallow sea. "The Archangel routs whole armies," I say. "He contends with the Devil."

"So it's said."

I feel my stare harden on nothing—there's air and shadows, nothing else. I should not be pretending that something's there. But I've known the Archangel to darken and enlarge even the most insignificant occurrences on his day, everyone seizing upon portents. When I lived in Palermo there was a boy I did not like whose birthday fell on Michaelmas, and I pitied him; his family wished him ill the way others wish their children good fortune, opportunity—because he was born, they insisted, to vanquish evil, and they were ambitious for him. He was a stiff, morose kid, ruined for life.

Even Scripture ascribes too much to the Archangel, it seems, the very omission of his name from texts implying conflicts taking place within his vast presence, as if he were the battlefield itself and the torn sky above, the very arena of combat. The Archangel leads the great battles for heaven at the beginning and end of time; he rescues the souls of the dying from the power of Satan; he is the champion of God's people, the patron of the Church and of the orders of knights; he calls men's souls away from earth and brings them to judgment.

The *benandanti* will remember all of this on the night of the battles. They'll amplify their dreams to accommodate the occasion—how could they not? What else do they have to guide them, after all? Their confused dreams, the windy confabulations of grandparents and aged hired help? And then there's the Archangel—martial, savage, benevolent, presiding over vast engagements between Good and Evil. The parallels for the *benandanti* are too self-serving, the opportunity for self-aggrandizement and all its trappings too attractive to resist.

Chiesa doesn't need this kind of psychic excess in his vitiated state. He's messed up enough as it is.

"Don't read too much into it, *Professoressa*," he tells me now.

"Not me," I say. "You."

He straightens up. I'm to think that mere annoyance has revived him, that his exhaustion is not profound. But he keeps a hand low on the wall behind him, dislodging shelly grit, his body propped out toward me.

"You take this much too seriously," he says. "Have you forgotten? I will be freed of this at forty, if I wish it! I haven't long. I'm thirty-eight—nearly thirty-nine years old—" He doubles over, coughs heavily into his fist, comes up flushed and argumentative. "Don't you think I can weather this, keep it in perspective? It's not a life sentence!"

I've put a hand out to steady him. I take a step back. It had been eight years or more, Giuseppe Gisira had testified, since he'd participated in the battles—I'd read that among the papers hidden in Chiesa's rooms. It was true: he'd been freed of his duty.

But Giuseppe Gisira had stood there in chains with those words in his mouth, still readily complicit and fully indictable, pinned by the inquisitor's grim interest and still saying *I am a benandante* and *I go with the others to fight*, even after so many years. He'd never even tried to argue that his long retirement from the battles should excuse him; he couldn't even crate his words up in past tense to make them seem less incriminating.

Chiesa pushes himself upright, dusts his hands. With that bit of fastidiousness he parts company with all the other sorry things that end up against walls like this, dazed old men, dogs, the victims of firing squads.

"All right, then," I say. "Let's move on."

But he stands a moment longer, as if the file of scaly old *portone* subsiding downhill were an arresting view; he's still trying to catch his breath.

I think of the Masuccio women—the widow and two daughters, beaked like birds—closing their beach house for the season. The light has receded from the tall pink rooms; they're dusky and oppressive now, their ceilings dark. A workman the women don't know nails shutters over the windows, his eyes calculating the value and portability of the rugs they've rolled, the chandelier they've bagged. Imperious and armed with nothing but the staring guile of children, they've imposed their helplessness upon him—and paid him only for his work. He will loot the house when they are gone.

The beach is an empty bed, grey and rumpled, the warmth of bodies long out of it. The women don't acknowledge the boarded villas around them, the gardens already loose from several weeks of neglect. They shroud the furniture, upend all the glassware. There has been no discussion of where they might go. Their limited wisdom decrees that they can't stay here: rumors of desperation must be thrown off by mobility, financial troubles by extravagance. People are starting to talk.

There are qualities of light now, myriad effects of illumination and shadow that lend theater to these last days, and I fall under their influence. The sun has come out of the earth and withdrawn to the sky; the library's golden, encrusted face is lit to advantage now, like a museum piece. The cobbled streets, the tiny, dark green parks dense with ornamental palms, the old furniture in shop windows take on a valedictory sheen: they're all moving toward an irretrievable past, a motion visible only to me. I'm waiting like one chosen to step forward with my packed bag and outlaw tactics when it all comes down, when Chiesa is fired and he falls like one stabbed on the street. I imagine catching him as he goes down, hustling him to his car and driving at life-saving, life-threatening speeds to some safehouse, where I rehabilitate him on a short course of anomie and sociopathic behavior. I believe I have a grasp of matters, a clear eye.

I have no idea. No idea at all.

Vergone's restless, knowing shade has returned again lately, too, haunting the edges of my vision when my eyes are on Chiesa. At least in this case I know why—or I think I do.

Chiesa lies on my unmade bed in his clothes and watches me now with Vergone's speculative gaze, exercising the right of the chronically ill to study others without compunction. It's my foreignness that intrigues him now, it seems, the things that make me strange to him. It isn't new, this prurient interest in my shaved legs and bathing habits; his illness and our ongoing carnality make him careless of propriety.

He compares me to Sabrina in these moments, I know he does—I feel her like a contradictory shadow next to me, straddling the bidet where I will not, sponging her limbs while I draw a razor down mine. It hasn't helped him to see her each week. She wants nothing from him but his *benandante* act, no small talk or even an injudicious rush of words she can cut off. He longs to embarrass himself with her in this way; she only wants the voodoo. He's bitter with me now sometimes, so suddenly that I'm taken by surprise and he draws blood. But he'll say anything when this happens—more than he means to. Like a cracked vessel, he's begun to leak what he contains.

Couched there on my bed, slit-eyed and obscurant, he asks me if all American women are as unclean as I. I've stripped for the second shower of the day; my skin feels gritty again, my hair heavy.

"It's your country that's so dirty," I say. "Half your soil is in the air—you could plow and plant it. I have to keep washing it off so it doesn't stick."

His thin smile doesn't waver; he seems to sink further into the bed.

"Such a Turk," he says. "How will you ever shift for yourself among us, if you insist upon all your strange ways?"

I've converted my irritation to motion, snatching up scattered clothes, crumpling them to my face to check for odors. Everything smells of sweat.

"I'm not staying here," I say. "I'm not working with the Council's shill."

There's a sudden silence like a clearing that I've blundered into, still thrashing and cursing under my breath.

"Where are you going, then?" Chiesa says.

Caught out I stare at him, my face prickling. I've taken us so far down the road to ruin together in my thoughts that I've forgotten: he doesn't know my plan. I haven't told him yet.

"Back to Providence, I guess," I tell him. Even when I need the casual lie, I can't call it home.

But here is where he stumbles. If he were still himself, if he were still even the drug-attenuated, well-turned-out figure I met three months ago, he'd never make this mistake. He wears the slighting, intemperate smile of a bureaucrat who's read my file.

"But who will take you in there?" he says.

I go into the bathroom, shut the door and bathe carelessly, languidly, sponging water down my back and onto the floor. The water steams and then goes tepid; I find my razor and shave my legs smooth, frowning over my memory of Chiesa's furtive interest in them, his tendency to stroke my shaved legs in little circles with his fingertips, as if checking for imperfections.

I've never told him that I left Providence a fugitive.

The improbable, the inconceivable, blooms abruptly in orchid colors; there are engines, stairways, machinery in giant halls that I'd thought were mere conceits.

Chiesa's known about me all along.

The razor slips from my fingers, strikes the floor. The ejected blade seals itself to the wet tiles.

Revelation is always the same, a sickening plunge. You never get used to it. There's the kick of panic, the sudden massing of past moments in a translating light—all at once they show teeth, those moments you'd thought innocuous, they bear critical inscriptions you should have read. It feels like grief, this sudden knowledge, a terrible regret.

He's never asked me what classes I teach, or my opinion of my students. He's never inquired about my teaching load, what I require of my students, the texts I use, the structure of my academic year, salary, pedagogy, grading systems— nothing. I'd taken this for self-absorption, a preoccupation with his own troubles, or the unquestioning esteem the world affords all American academics. I'd thought it a piece of damned good luck, best left undisturbed.

And the casual scrutiny he's turned on me lately that reminds me of Vergone—Vergone, who's sized me up and knows I'm good for nothing but a fight. Chiesa knows it, too.

The grey tiles weep moisture; sweat runs into my eyes and burns like tears. Why am I here, then? Why has he let me run this scam of mine if he knew I was useless to him, if he knew that I could never advance his archives' fortunes?

The bathroom door cracks the tiled wall, shudders on its hinges. I've wound myself in a damp bath sheet that grips me like seaweed and I fling out into the bedroom shouting *Chiesa, you shit, what have you—*

But of course he's already gone.

CHAPTER TWENTY-FOUR

He's invisible to me for days then, an illusionist's deliberate work, moving just out of my sight in the hotel. He puts landings between us on the stairs, hugs the wall as he climbs. He leaves air marked with his breath, the smell of his hair eddying in hallways, and I pass through it like turbulence, gasping, staring for its source. He passes through doors behind me, treads the carpets ahead; lights go on and off in his rooms.

I can't solve the puzzle of what I'd do were I to catch him out in this. His disappearance—and now this strange haunting—have undone me; he'll have taken on some terrible aspect, I think, Cerberus' stare, now that he's past dissembling. I'm afraid to see him so changed. I'd gone down the hall after him in a fury, the bath sheet's wet hem chafing my ankles, but he must have known that I wouldn't get far; by the time I reached the disused stairs to his rooms I knew myself for what I was, a hypocrite staging sub-par theatrics. Draped like some drama club's notion of a minor goddess, thin-skinned and ill-tempered, I wished abruptly to be out of myself, away. I'd crept back to my rooms willing all doors to stay closed, no one to see me.

Chiesa vanishes like smoke, he falls away from me like a screen. I peer into grey revealed space and see that there's been hidden intent in all his dealings with me, a single iron purpose like a scaffold from which he's flown multiple effects: confidences, journeys of instruction, mutual seduction. My whole stay here has been rigged by Valparuta's archivist, even as I'd thought my own game was running.

My months in Valparuta stand open, littered like a struck stage. I inspect them now for devices, the means by which Chiesa led me.

The *benandanti's* trials, hidden but marked like treasure. He'd let accident deliver Piero Quagliata to me, but the rest—the coded file box, de Quincey's riddling text—was all his doing, a salting of clues. Afterwards I'd said to him *You meant those trials to be found*; *not everyone would have found them*, he'd replied. It had been a test, then—an experiment in the workings of chance and then of my own fierce tendencies, my habits of pursuit. If I'd let that curious scene at Piero Quagliata's house pass unre-marked, if my stores of knowledge had failed me or I'd bent to Chiesa's resistance, would the archivist have taken me up as he did? Would I have travelled with him into the countryside, seen the Cadmus and the fall of the Masuccio, passed into Risacca's hands? Would he have let me take him that first time and then again and again, would I have known about the wounds he sus-tained from empty air, his dreams of night travel and contested harvests, his self-contempt, his broken heart? Would he have pressed my sightedness on me, even as he closed his own eyes to the fraud I'd perpetrated on him?

Chiesa is neither innocent nor complicit in what I've done to him, I realize; he'd been pursuing his own ends.

The desk clerk deals yellow registration cards out before her like tarot, a line of six and then others atop them, face up and face down. I watch her like a cardsharp but I can't divine her system.

She ignores the ringing phone. "The mayor took *pastina* yesterday," she says. "His blood has cleared." She studies the cards on the desk, places the card in her hand deliberately.

"Cleared?" I touch a yellow stack. "Why does it go there?"

"Don't you see? The same ink is used on this one and that one." She lays the next card crosswise on the last, confounding me. "Yes, the doctor took three tubes and went away content. The week before he'd flung the tube he'd drawn away from him."

"Surprised him, eh?" I know it's old women's gossip but I partake anyway.

"Well, it was black, you know, the blood! He suspected contamination, a dangerous trick of some kind. He left in a fury."

"What do they say now—the mayor will live?"

"No, but the *benandante* has laid hold of him; they're contending for his soul."

There seems no end to the registration cards. They bloom in her fingers like sleight-of-hand; the overburdened stacks slump, run into each other. Vexed, I look away.

But the Elimo itself must be in on the trick—signs of a crowd's heavy passage, a reason for all those cards, are everywhere. The lobby carpets need sweeping, the wastebaskets brim with crumpled tissues and paper cups; the smell of smothered grease fires and dishwasher vapor hangs in the restaurant doorway. Hundreds of invisible conventioneers seem to have come and gone in some unbookable, unverifiable interstitium, disarranging cushions, spilling drinks, snapping the fronds of the potted palms. The place looks unkempt, overused.

"Where have they come from, all these guests? I haven't seen them."

The desk clerk shrugs. "They've come and gone, *Professoressa.*"

"You don't get their mailing addresses? For billing purposes?" I reach out, turn a stack of registration cards to read them. She makes no move to stop me.

The cards are all written with saints' names, and prayers for their intercession. *Against my enemies' plots, St. Drausius protect me*, I read. *St. Rita with your roses and figs, spare me my loneliness.* I toss them in like a bad hand.

"I wish to report an incident," I say. "The archivist has taken advantage of me, and now has gone into hiding."

Her brows rise fractionally; her fingers crimp the stacks of cards back into place. "He has made advances—?"

"No, no, that was all my doing." I'm nickel-plated on this subject, her icepick look skitters off me. "No, he's set out to influence me without my knowledge—he's taken me places and shown me things I did not want to see."

"Well, perhaps he is just a poor host," she says. "Or you are a difficult guest."

I take her wrist then, stop her hand. The card she holds reads *St. Ubaldus, rid me of my demons.* "He has administered a course of instruction, Signorina," I say. "He has brought me along for his own purposes."

She lets her wrist lie in my grasp. "Can he not be a bit overzealous, *Professoressa*? Must you insist upon assuming the worst? He has great hopes for your work here—"

"But he doesn't," I say. "He doesn't. He knew when I arrived that I was finished in academia. I haven't written anything in years. Even if I could—and I can't, it's all left me—no one would publish it now."

Somewhere upstairs a door closes softly. I've gone and told her too much, the sorry facts that no one can help. It's a mistake like falling in dreams, a mishandling of the self; it shocks me like a real fall.

The desk clerk's gaze flickers; she seems to view me from a distance. "You are not a scholar, then."

"I'm telling you, it didn't matter to him."

"You can do nothing to promote his archives."

"He knew this. He knew it. It wasn't what he wanted from me."

She frees herself from my grip then, deliberately; she might be shedding an accessory she no longer cares for. "Why did you come here, then?"

She expects my reaction, watches me shift angrily and then fail to walk away from her. She's seen it before, thwarted guests discovering that they have nowhere else to turn.

"You wish to lodge a complaint, *Professoressa?*" she says.

I find myself thinking of all his strange bones, tented up under skin I thought I recognized. "Yes," I say.

"Then you must tell me the circumstances surrounding your dissatisfaction." She takes up a pen, turns a registration card on its face. "And so?" she says. "Why did you come here?"

"To get away, okay?" I say. "To see these archives."

The pen contacts the paper, travels sharply downward.

"Why are you the only one?" She's drawing fractals, the veins of leaves.

"What?"

"Why are there no other scholars? Surely others have applied."

A young guy bumps through the kitchen's swinging doors, his elbows a mash of pink scars from years of soccer played on stony lots. He looks like he knows I've been stupid as a cow in sunshine all this time; he glares at me from under his flanged helmet of overlong hair, slams down a rack of glassware and stalks back to his pots and pans.

Well, he's right to be pissed, I think. I should have figured this out long ago. Because that flimsy brochure from Valparuta's Commission for Cultural Resources would have wound up in other faculty mailboxes on other campuses; it would have been pinned up on other departmental corkboards already shaggy with outdated notices and it would have been read, its aberrant syntax and oilslick colors attracting a certain breed of academic—the microhistorian, the goofball, the cultural anthropologist. I can stand here right now with the desk clerk's eyes pushing me like a wind and off the top of my head think of two or three people who'd apply, who'd kill to come here on sabbatical. And all of them—even the woman who finds coded references to diabolism in Giuseppe Pitrè's early cultural studies—would have had more business here than I.

The archivist had turned down all other applicants.

The desk clerk watches this news reach me like water thrown in my face, the pen still moving of its own accord, her fingers only holding it upright in its travels. The pen shades in a fine rain of strokes, lays down a muscular line, and in the inverted image (Rorschach, Rorschach) I think I see the *Commissione*—that vague, impostor body—scattering crumbs and cigarette ashes over a half-dozen baffling CVs and letters of intent before sending them on to Chiesa.

He'd rejected them all out of hand, probably on bogus criteria the *Commissione* never bothered to examine. All but mine.

The desk clerk is drawing vast hanging gardens on a tiny scale now, filling the card with trailing vines. I say something to her, *The programme was only ever for me, to bring me here*—those words or their approximates, but my mouth feels numb and my fingers are buzzing like locusts; it's not enough to draw her away from what she's doing.

The trip up to my rooms is a staged climb into thinning air, and so I camp on the landing for a bit, gasping, the *Guerrièra's* razor smile over my shoulder. From that modest height I can see where it all started, a tiny ragged moment like a ship afire on the horizon's curved edge, and I wonder how I've missed it all along.

That newspaper clipping in my faculty mailbox, creased to fit a small envelope.

"Vergone." The hotel payphone's mouthpiece smells like a spittoon; its narrow steel privacy wings do not protect me. "Vergone," I say, "that Friday in the hallway."

It's morning there, the fall term's just begun and I've taken him by surprise; I can hear his confusion, the little glottal stops as he misses his verbal footing once, twice. He's making toast, I think; his damp hair has spoiled the cleaners' starch job on his collar. I know him like this, ramped up for teaching. Well-pressed and still smelling of soap, his blade edges are just starting to wear through. "There was a Friday?" he says.

"In the hallway, just you and me. A snowstorm coming in. You remember?"

"Should I?"

"You decided to tell me about these archives."

A dead voice of irony. "Right there, I decided. In the hallway."

"Tell me I'm wrong."

This time there's nothing, a hiatus of indrawn breath—and nothing.

"I'd gone past you, Vergone. You had nothing to say to me. And then you called me back."

"So—what?" he says. "What?"

"What did I do?"

Again, little choking sounds. I can just see him, going for the kitchen window like he wants to climb out and then leaning there, stymied, peering at the nursery-grown saplings on the street's verge, the parked cars. "You think you did something? You did something, and then I decided, 'what the fuck, just for that, I'll tell her'?"

"Or I didn't—maybe I didn't—" I have to start over. "I shouldn't have been there. I should have been staying away."

"Well, sure. Instead of showing up every day like the fucking Red Death. Casting a pall on the festivities."

"Yes."

There's a long silence. I listen to an electrical wind.

"Vergone?"

I hear him come back to me, an ocean sound. His tone is changed. "They're just about done with you, by the way," he says. "You'll be getting a letter."

"Okay."

"I could—"

"No, don't," I say, to make him stop. "It's okay."

The Elimo's darkened lobby waits like a stage set, all artifact. It's two in the morning here; there could be air, bedrock, ocean depths beyond the hotel's black windows.

"It wasn't you," Vergone says. "You didn't do anything. I just remembered it right then, that article. I'd been meaning to mention it to you."

"Liar," I say and I can hardly breathe; it's like he's breaking my heart, as if I could be so easily injured. "Jesus, Vergone—"

"Joan—"

I can feel him forming phrases meant to deter me; he thinks a little cajolery will defuse the moment, the kind of fond abuse that works on spooky horses and overwrought women. I tell him to shut up. I tell him that Chiesa had sent him that clipping weeks before—hadn't he?—weeks before, with instructions to press it on me. Not just pass it on but press it on me, make sure that I'd read it. And if that didn't set me ablaze and launch me like a roman candle toward Valparuta, what then? What was the contingency plan? More badgering? More casual endorsements in the hallway, *I dunno, looked pretty interesting, your kind of thing, get away from here maybe, let this mess play out*—? Would he have shown up one day at my ransacked closet of an office with one of those flimsy brochures and some story of how he'd obtained it?

"Never worried about it," Vergone says. He's going to make me pay for this, for making him own up. "I saw what you were doing, showing up every day like that, looking for trouble. Trying to get yourself thrown out. You wanted to get it over with."

"That's why you did it."

I hear the blunt sound of him juggling the handset. He's letting me go. I'm caught between his shoulder and ear now, he's freed up his hands to take hold of the morning's delayed business, the cooling toast, the scattered papers, the shirtcuffs he'll unbutton and roll to his elbows. He's been sheltering me, I think he believes that—he's been kind to me without my knowledge, and now he's done with it. The lenses of his glasses flash like little silver fish.

"The look on your face, Joan," he tells me. "In the hallway. If you'd had a knife, you'd have put it in my hands and run on it."

He's drawing away, I feel it, and I clutch the heavy payphone to my ear to hold him for just a little longer. He'd held off—Chiesa had sent him that clipping but Vergone had held off giving it to me, waiting to see if I'd save myself, maybe, waiting to see if I'd even bother to try. He'd given me the means to a more decorous exit only when he saw that I was determined to go down hard.

"Vergone," I say and something catches in my chest, too late to acknowledge; I can't prevail upon him now. "Vergone," I say, "what does he want me for?"

And for the first time he speaks to me in Italian, in the rusty, blunt cadences of a Palermitan teen.

"Ask my cousin," Vergone says. "He will tell you now."

CHAPTER TWENTY-FIVE

For two days I stumble about as if pursued by wasps, arms over my head; Chiesa remains out of sight. I can go no further than the places he might be, the library, the hotel, the twisting alleys and shadowed doorways between.

There's a perimeter of shattered nests, eggshells, caulks of birdshit and dead fledglings around the library now. The doors are locked, there's an unlit gloom beyond them and a few blighted ficus leaves like curled blades on the vestibule floor. The Council has seized the building, ordered this apocalyptic sweeping of its cornices; the rock pigeons' wholesale death announces Chiesa's impending fall.

He will not show himself. He's reached across an ocean, used his cousin Vergone to bait and hook me like a fish—a medieval plot, at once cunning and absurd. It should not have worked. Yet here I am, just wakened to my own abduction; and all at once my very body is suspect, something I want to part from, to reconsider at a safe distance. I no longer trust myself.

Chiesa knows me where I do not. I want to consult him like an oracle.

And finally it comes to me, what I have to do to bring him out. I take a table in the Elimo's bar and start in on their single malt.

It's a room like a corridor, dark, too narrow for the bad translation of British clubbiness wedged into it. I've fallen into a plaid wingbacked chair whose padded sides blinker me like a cart horse; the barman brings me a double and a glass of still water only because he has not yet decided how he will rid the place of me. He returns to the bar but I feel his eyes on my bare legs, all he can see of me in this ridiculous chair. I cross my knees, let one shoe slip from my heel.

He's back much too soon, a busybody, a would-be perpetrator.

"I'll take another," I say, and lift my glass on my palm. There's still an inch of oily liquid in it, tilting.

He tells me no, he's sorry but there is no more, a terrible oversight but he has nothing in reserve; he tries to pluck the glass from my hand. I let him tug briefly at it before sheltering it again in my lap.

"No, no, this fruit's not ready to fall, Signor," I say, and give him my best smile. "A companion will be joining me soon—can I help it if he's left me compromised in the meantime?"

"I will inform him, *Professoressa*, that you've returned to you rooms."

"But I haven't returned to them. I'm having a drink."

The barman's blank tomcat face goes sour. The women of his family—mother, sisters, aunts—must labor daily to smooth his path, I think; his good looks spoil too easily, with unsightly results. He searches the empty train car of a room for something to use against me.

"You may as well bring me another," I say. "Things will only get worse if you don't."

The barman's eyes widen. He can't quite believe this incident that feels, perversely, like good fortune; he wants to say *No, you don't mean it, do you?* before putting me resoundingly in my place. But Chiesa stands behind him now, too close, bouncer close, an offer of bodily harm confided like a secret. Irises fully eclipsed, he waits for the barman to step aside.

"Never mind her, Mimmo," he says. "I tell you, she'll leave you with your balls in your hands."

The barman sputters, searches Chiesa's face for a disavowal of such an outrageous claim, but nothing comes; the archivist may have only words and gestures left to him right now, the automaton's limited gifts, as the drug he's on carries him out of sensibility's reach.

"Go tend your bar," Chiesa says. "I'll see to her." He appears to check the barman's shirt pocket for its contents, leaves several bills there. "Bring her another. And me as well."

I miss him already, I find, the superseded Chiesa—this new one seems larger, and simplified, missing those edges that caught the most light. He takes a cowhide club chair not quite opposite me, a seat big and precarious as the steer itself might have offered in life, and he seems easy there, a good fit for it; I'm left to regard the side of his face, the view I'd have if he were conversing with someone else.

"This will get around," he says.

"Then you should have come sooner." I spoil my fresh drink with the dregs of the first, set the empty glass down hard. He's been in the walls, I think, watching; what he knows of me has cost him nothing yet.

"There were melons on doorsteps this morning, stuck full of glass." Chiesa swallows a mouthful of scotch, lips curling. "It can't come soon enough, an end to this."

"There's no end," I say. "The Advent Embertide will come, and the Lenten Embertide, and the Whit Embertide—"

"This one will end. Each one ends."

I turn away from him, irritated, for a view of my chair's fake regimental plaid. It's flattened him out, this tension between his wish for an end to these night battles—for Michaelmas Thursday to come no matter the mortal shame he will incur—and his dread of all the unlibraried, unarchived days that will follow. He's grown dull with it; there's a worthless fidelity to him now, a useless candor. What can he tell me, except that he can't see past this Thursday, that today is Tuesday already and the hours are eroding like stone? What can he do but blow like a circuit if he hears what I have planned for this doubtful future, a career of repeated misdemeanors and compulsive flight?

Leave that, I tell myself, leave it. The whiskey warms me like a sweater I wish I could put off.

"Vergone did it for me, not you," I say. "The clipping thing."

Chiesa knows this; his nod only acknowledges my arrival at the truth. "He and I were never close," he says.

But I would have said the same, had anyone pressed me about Vergone. The error seems unforgivable now, a falsehood told for convenience. I close my eyes and something ironbound leaves me; I feel myself coming apart, cracking like joinery. For years I've told myself that I do not prevaricate, ever—that I see the scratches and dents I put in the world, that I do not love myself. I thought I held a sword over my own head.

"What did you tell him, Chiesa, when he asked you what it was for?"

He doesn't want to tell me, goes on a casual hunt through his clothes for a cigarette—and his motions ignite in me an unbearable longing to touch him, as if he were dead and gone, already beyond my reach.

"He was doing me a favor, he thought," I say. "What did you tell him?"

"That it was a rare opportunity. For one with your background."

"My background in interpreting Renaissance material wealth." I sound just like Vergone, my voice flat, discrediting. "My background in surveying probate inventories."

"Yes, of course. Why not?"

"And then he told you. That I was not as advertised."

"He did, yes. But it didn't matter."

I think of Vergone's tinny, circumspect apologies for me, ravelled out over transatlantic distances. He'd have barely remembered this Sicilian cousin of his from grandparents' funerals before his family's emigration to the States—just one of a dozen boys unhappy in good clothes, struck silent in the midst of blood strangers. Vergone would have let whole minutes of ionized silence buzz down the telephone line, trying to comprehend his cousin's peculiar indifference to his warnings.

Chiesa is worrying a crushed pack of Gauloises. "You had other, more relevant credentials, *Professoressa*," he says. "But my cousin would not have understood them."

There are prints of British racehorses on the walls, mythical beasts with human eyes and bodies like furniture, pedigrees of biblical length. I fix my swimming gaze on them. "My mother," I say.

He's extracted a cigarette from the mangled pack, puts it between his lips. "What do you call the capacities you have? The character defects? Not your inheritance."

"No—"

It's come out of me like a cry. He gives me a swift, sympathetic look, returns to the business of getting a smoke.

"No, you could have chosen otherwise. And yet she was a kind of force majeur, your mother. Even her absence affected the weather. Her death brought down trees."

I am no more capable of tears than a crocodile, my blood is thick and slow in my veins but that doesn't stop me from seeing it, trees down like scythed grain, a blast measured in megatons. I fend the image off. "You don't know. You don't know," I say.

"No," he replies, "I don't know. But look at you."

I sit there helpless in the skin that I cannot put off, furious with him—him and Vergone and their damnable plans for me, the use they thought they could make of me.

"What's wrong with you, Chiesa? You think you have to get Simona Origo's daughter, that no one else can do whatever it is that you want done? You think she's got some kind of mark on her?"

"Yes."

"What is it? What is it?"

"I don't know. I've been completely wrong about you. And yet there's no one else."

He'd imagined me some fantastic hybrid, I think—a new and more viable species, impervious to history. "Tell me why you brought me here," I say.

"To show you all of this. To put it before you."

"It's nothing to me. The minute you're gone, I'm walking away."

But he doesn't seem to hear. A faint smile softens his face; he may be thinking of all the vital records and court documents he'd unearthed in pursuit of me, the pleasure of wielding his formidable research skills. "Your name was changed," he says.

Russell changed it, when I went to him.

The smoke from Chiesa's cigarette hangs plumb in the air; he passes a hand through it. "I'll never call you Joan," he says.

So he must have meant my presence here as a corrective, a counterbalance to his own necessary failings of discipline and reason; Valparuta's archivist had invoked me like some patron saint. He's vague now on the specifics of how I was to intercede for him. Like most blown schemes its logic has escaped its creator first; he'll say only that it was indecent, the lengths she went to, the risks she ran. He asks me *How does one survive a mother as powerful and ridiculous as yours?* before he rolls away from me, dragging the bedclothes with him. He doesn't know that I've acquired a purpose of my own, independent of the strange, disparaging hagiography he's assigned me; he thinks I've failed him like some lesser saint. I lie where he's left me, pressed into the bed like an open hand, incapable of taking offense. I have us on the car ferry at Messina, the Lancia in the hold among freight trucks with smoking tires and banks of amber running lights, the two of us climbing metal gangways to the dingy café topside, dizzy with the smells of diesel exhaust and marine paint. I put us at the ferry's rail, taking in Messina's low white profile, the thump of the noon cannon; I have us see the flash of sunlight as the gilt clockwork Christ in the Duomo's campanile ticks up from his sepulchre.

Those will be the good days, while our actions still seem those of a holiday escapade, the first thefts done on dares and wagers between us. I imagine these days glittering with dust, sunk like monuments in sand.

Chapter Twenty-Six

So it comes, Michaelmas Thursday. It opens and plays like cinema, beautiful and entirely prefigured, even its seeming uncertainties wholly contrived. Everything on the street and within rooms speaks, it's all emblem; the day advances like a treatise.

In chambers with a painted tympanum the City Council drafts Chiesa's termination notice. Charity, Industry and Knowledge recline, distorted, on the ceiling above them, attended by tiny creatures with human eyes—mice and nightjars, stag beetles, snakes. No official commentary exists to explain this curious rendering, the work of some assiduous hack who began in the style of Tiepolo and ended in apparent delirium. The Council quarrels fiercely only over the terms of Chiesa's severance, how little they can leave him with. They are vindictive as women, draped like pageant contestants in their sashes of office. They do not consult the mayor. But when the Council chair peers out into the hall in search of a courier there's Emedio, Agretta's aide, lounging against the wall, fingering the crease in his trousers. He proves obdurate as fate itself in his delivery of bad news, there's no stopping him, no amending his near-teleologic indifference. He stands there at the door of Chiesa's flat and says *So I guess this place will be vacant soon*, taking in the ocher walls and plaster moldings over the archivist's shoulder. *Does it have a good big bathtub?* He dances clear of the kick Chiesa sends after him, takes the stairs down two at a time, out into a wind that tries like a smitten girl to pull his suitcoat from his shoulders.

It's an heraldic day, armies of towering clouds in the sky, their racing shadows blooming and fading on walls. I take Chiesa by the sleeve and lead him outside, into this day lit like an arena and he comes along stunned, robbed of volition. I've come upon him ministering to himself, sitting on the side of his bed that's been made up and empty for days, leaning over the needle in his arm as if in shared confidence. He's called me in on my knock at his door, he doesn't care what I see—or he does, and this is further argument on the subject of his blighted cause. It doesn't matter. I get him up, I find his sunglasses and his keys. He's left the Lancia in the tiny piazza the hotel has appropriated for a parking lot, wedged in among cars parked like cattle in a corral; it's picked up a long red crease in its right rear quarter-panel. I take the tire iron from the Lancia's trunk, Chiesa standing off like a tree in the foreground. Down a long dim cul-de-sac a dumpster burns with a smell of animal sacrifice, scorched hair and bone. A woman on the street lets her shopping fall from her hands, sniffs the air with the face of one reading words, wine vinegar pooling at her feet. I have to pull Chiesa away. He's reading, too, it seems—there's a profound absence about him. Through his sleeve I can feel where the needle's gone in. I like the weight of the tire iron in my hand; I swing it experimentally.

So when I put it through a library window it's like I've been breaking and entering all along, only this time there are shards of glass involved, an indecorous climb onto a stone buttress. I've thought to wrap the head of the tire iron in a rag but I can't be bothered; I've left Chiesa nodding, unattended, at a rear service door. There's still a saw's edge of broken glass in the sill when I climb through and I cut my knee on it, a long shallow gash that fills with blood like the crease in the Lancia's side. I let myself down into the women's restroom, kick a wicker stand stacked with paper towels out of the way of my fall.

Chiesa's taken a piss meantime in the service door's stairwell, a dark fan of wetness on the wall and a yeasty smell that he's already disowned; he's turned his back on it, waiting with his face pressed to the door and his arms crossed as if against cold. He shoulders me out of the way, slips inside and shuts the door softly, softly—he's not as high as he seems, and yet when I lead him upstairs to the archives and invite him to take what's due him he stands with his hands hanging at his sides, gone elsewhere and swaying slightly on his feet, as if he were rooted underwater.

"They've severed you without pay," I tell him. "You're going to need some capital."

"No," he sighs.

"You will," I say.

"Maybe," he says. "But I'm not doing this."

"They've screwed you, Chiesa. And who knows what's going to happen to this place now? It's in the hands of shysters—things will be stolen and misfiled, they won't monitor the climate control. You may as well salvage something— it'll be safer with you no matter where you are."

But he only looks at me as if I were one of those manuscripts myself, my words of historic interest alone, entirely artifactual.

"Then I'll do it," I say.

"You may as well," Chiesa replies. "Every day you spent in my archives was a crime committed."

"Yes," I say. "And you knew it, too."

A fluorescent tube howls in the archives' ceiling now, stuttering like a lit fuse; the heaps of books and file boxes burying my desk have settled into a geology of their own. I've come in here to plunder what I'd already gathered up—the steel door slams behind me as if I really were the Council's nemesis, come to perpetrate some dubious act of vigilantism. But I find that I can't mine these massed ranges of books and papers for value, I can't strip off their peaks—it's all mother lode to me, all hard as rock. I'd have to take it all. Stymied, I stand over the desk and read what I'd last written, weeks ago: *three spoons of horn, a dry firkin, a doublet of undyed wool.*

I didn't survive my mother. This is where Chiesa went wrong—I've been dying of her all along. I won't outlast the sale of the Cadmus and the de Quincey by much. Their theft was the end of my brief ability to choose the loss of one thing over another; when the money from those two books runs out I'll be done intervening in the natural death of anything. Chiesa and I will have a short run then, months only—the natural lifespan of the smallest creatures.

So I figure I should find him quickly, take him up as something precious and short-lived; the night battles will discharge like lightning in any case, independent of anyone's wishes. I can caress him, attend him, distract him all I want until he sleeps, and in the morning while he fumbles after the fragments of his dreams I'll pack that handled canvas bag and we'll leave.

He's deep in the stacks on the top floor, in Applied Sciences; he holds a small volume of engineering principles to his face.

He asks the book: "What did you take, then?"

"Nothing," I tell him. "I can't leave any of it behind."

He nods. "That sickness of yours," he says. "It's nearly ruined you."

"I broke glass to get us in here, Chiesa. And now it's like we're made of wood, we can't even help ourselves."

"I can't even hear you," he says, "that's the problem. There's been a roaring in my ears all day. I can't think."

"Then let's make Mimmo sell us a bottle," I say. "We'll make it so Emedio won't want your flat."

A look of fugitive, scabrous appetite crosses his face; he slots the book back into place. "I have a tray of *dolci*," he says like a proposition.

So we'll have alcohol and sweets, I think; we can darken Chiesa's rooms and stay on there for the rest of the day, as if abandoned by our better parts.

"Come on, then," I say.

And that's what it's like, a deliberate abandonment—it's the impending night battles that have suspended us like flags in still air, but we let it look like degeneracy, a leaving off of higher purpose. In his absence Chiesa's rooms have taken on a limestone smell of vacancy; we come in yawning, kicking off shoes, tugging at our clothes. Mimmo's given us a bad American bourbon, the evil, resiny stuff he feeds the drunks. Chiesa sets it on the table like a prize. Something's gotten into the tray of marzipan in the kitchenette—the candies seem disturbed, awry in their lace paper cups; some are pocked with holes. It's the heat, Chiesa says carelessly, rinsing glasses in the sink. They've been sitting out for days. He's forgotten his claims of infestation, of biting vermin in the walls.

Outside the day thunders like a foundry, throwing off successive waves of heat and tungsten light. I hear metallic voices but can see no one conversing; a teetering chimney of stained produce boxes has appeared in the kitchen courtyard below us. I close all the wooden shutters, a marzipan carrot sticky in my fingers.

We occupy the long twilight afternoon with killing off the bourbon, picking through the suspect marzipan. We go to bed for perfunctory sex, get up again, share a cigarette that tastes like the floor of a dry forest. No topic of discussion seems safe; at one point as the room begins to darken we bicker like parliamentarians over the correct cut of meat for *carne aglassata*. We're in need of a proper dinner, but we're preoccupied—and so the Embertide enforces the fasting of even the faithless, the unbelievers like us.

At last we switch on the lights, and it's a mistake; we can't avoid each other like this. Chiesa, all bones and dishevelment, stares at me in pity and consternation.

"What is it?" he says.

"What?" I say. "What?" Boozy, alarmed, I check my limbs and my belly for marks, bugs, old scars that might show livid in bad light.

"Your face," he says, "your poor thin arms—I hadn't noticed—"

"Noticed what? What?"

He wakens to his blunder, tries out of kindness to paper over it. "Nothing, nothing," he says. "It's my fault—you don't look quite yourself, that's all. I think I've just missed it until now."

"There's nothing wrong with me."

He won't say yes or no to this. "But you've cut yourself," he says.

"Oh, that," I say. I pinch up the skin on my knee to inspect the wound and it blanches, stings fiercely. "It just needs some iodine."

"That's all?"

I think he's suggesting holy water. I give him a withering look.

"I was thinking stitches," he says.

I put my face in my hands. "It doesn't need stitches," I say. "It's not very deep."

"All right, then."

He turns back to the bed for his shirt, and I understand from his careful buttoning and averted gaze that I should dress, too. I pull on the jersey dress I've worn all day; it smells of soot and effort, there's a bloodstain on its hem. It's getting dark at last, but there are hours yet until sleep—we'll never make it without another bottle, something more to eat.

There's no phone to call down to the desk, or to importune once again upon that sourpuss Mimmo. Chiesa stares at me defiantly. "I told them," he says. "When I took this place I told them that I was not on call. I was not their man."

"Great," I say. "So you couldn't trust yourself to just tell them to fuck off? You had to go without a phone?"

He shows his teeth like he's going to bite but his anger fails him; he hunches on the side of the bed, working his feet into shoes. "It won't hurt us to get out a bit," he says.

I shrug. "It won't hurt me," I say.

Yet it seems that I will always be subject to clandestine journeys out at night, into city streets, at the will of others. It's a prejudicial view, and I know it—I want more to drink and something to fill my queasy stomach, too—but I find that

I'm a casualty of Chiesa's sudden single-mindedness as he carries me headlong from one covert encounter to another.

Chiesa holds me against him and we rush into the dark, heads down as if through rain. We pass lit shops with dusty bottles in their windows, the aluminum glint of a *tavola calda* and its attendant aromas of fried *arancini* and olive brine. He tells me *No, not there*; instead he pulls me into black passageways and does business in the old manner, in shadowed doorways, wrapped packages and bottles twisted up in paper bags passed to him with handshakes, fierce embraces, a few murmured words.

It proves a stunning haul, laid out in its paper and foil wrappings on Chiesa's big old pedestal table. It's more than we could ever eat, and it comes to me that it's not food so much as tribute; it's meant to be wasted, like a sacrifice.

And there's something of the executioner's largesse in it, too—that big last dinner of fried chicken, potatoes, greens and pie a la mode you'd feed a field hand or a birthday boy that will fuel nothing, that will go entirely to waste. The *Valparuti* know their archivist is finished here. It's a sendoff into the next world, this giant spread, and they know that place will be a purgatory of strangers, a town in another province, perhaps, and empty of relations.

So we chew our way through the leftovers of a dozen *piatti vastasi*, the rich, heavy fare of Sicily's bourgeoisie—*maccheroni* with chicken livers, sausage *impanata*, an elaborate *tummala*, grilled *involtini* leaking veal sauce and melted cheese. We dig the corks out of three bottles of last year's homemade vintage and drink them down to their sediment, our gestures enlarging, our thoughts increasingly muddled. We lose all our circumspection, the wisdom that's kept us silent until now, and we confess, we confess, errant words spilling out of us, the kinds of things we should never say.

I wag my heavy head like some tiresome know-it-all. "I wouldn't see anything tonight, Chiesa," I say. "If I were to keep watch over you. The early stages of sleep are like dying—that's what these poor wakeful wives have been seeing all this time. Listen: their husbands' breathing slows, it stops and starts, their bodies cool. Those wives know what they're seeing; deathwatches and mortuary ritual have always been the province of women. And this lying like the dead— it's REM sleep, Chiesa, I'm telling you. You can die, you can dream, the same thing happens—your mouth falls open, your limbs stretch out and go still. No one can rouse you. Your body is dead and yet your closed eyes seem to be following some hectic action, you're breathing like a man in a fight. God has entered the room and brought with him this dreadful paradox—your soul's gone abroad in the service of Christ."

Chiesa stares at me, bemused. "I imagined you taller," he says. "I thought I'd see more of your father in you."

"So I won't see anything," I say again. "Nothing out of your mouth."

His chair scrapes back. "You've grown haggard," he says. "I can't help but think that these matters would never have troubled your mother and father."

He returns from the kitchen with a plastic shopping bag, shakes it out so that it bellies and collapses like a failed parachute, tips into it a sagging paper plate of uneaten beef *stracotto*.

"Agretta's recovering, you know," he says.

And then he throws everything away, the *scacciata* we never touched, the honey-soaked *sfinci* that would have travelled well, the slumping squares of *tiramisu* that might have done for breakfast. I don't try to stop him.

"Agretta eyes me like a shark now," Chiesa says. "He insists that my bathroom scale has saved him—he's bought all that rigamarole I staged in front of them. What a rube! I think he hates me now, for proving it of him. In a few weeks he'll be back to his speeches, and his rhetoric will swallow us again like a fogbank. But nothing will change. Anything new will be turned to old purposes, and we'll go on just as we are."

There's the rending, implosive sound of someone breaking down those boxes in the courtyard below, a barrage of insults and laughter. I follow the uproar indiscriminately, like a drunk in a crowded bar. Chiesa's table-clearing is disorganized now; he's moving to stay ahead of his thoughts.

"Sabrina looked at us like we were wearing skins, both of us," he says. "Like our gods had the heads of animals. I wanted to crawl into a corner and cut my own throat, seeing her face. I thought it was the bathroom scale that disgusted her—the gestures and improvised prayers I made, the ass her husband made of himself . . . but she'd brush me off like a spider whenever I turned to her, whenever I opened my mouth. She thinks it's ridiculous, contemptible, the way I still look at her . . . I may as well worship fire and carry stone tools, I offend her so badly with this old enthusiasm of mine—"

I take the dripping bag from him, turn him to me. I stroke his face the way Simona did mine, the way she did Russell's to impose her will on him.

"Where are your car keys, Chiesa?"

"You have them. I've left them with you."

And it's true, I remember; I have them in my purse. "Let's take a drive," I say.

"I'm in no shape to—now?"

"In the morning. The morning. I'll pack a bag."

"You know I'm short of cash."

"I know. I know."

I have a whole whispered litany of inflammatory promises at hand, everything I ever heard from my mother. I never knew I'd archived all those shiny, alloyed phrases.

"Let's go to bed," I say. "We'll make an early start."

There's a gecko like a bas-relief on the bedroom wall, a mayfly with tissue wings and trailing legs courting the lamp's incandescent bulb. We fall in a tangle of limbs and half-shed clothes into a bed that smells of clay, and sleep covers us like silt.

CHAPTER TWENTY-SEVEN

But then Chiesa leaves without me.

Donna Perchta, I've come to think, exercises the cruelty and dispatch of an Iron Age queen. I see her in a doeskin skirt and bodice; her short cloak of leopard-skin is secured with a bone fibula. She wears a totemic headdress, the caped-out head and horns of a fallow-deer set in a circlet of beaten gold. Fully imagined like this, armed and coifed and shod, she holds all my grief.

Those dreams that left me like a flock of starlings that morning—I'm thinking more and more that I remember them wheeling off in a great shifting, teeming body, my ears full of their noise. I don't know; others are working to convince me of it, glib as salesmen. What I do know is that I woke out of myself somehow, displaced; Chiesa's bed seemed strange to me, as if something else had lain down in it while I slept. Struck still by those departing dreams, I lay and felt the changed room and thought, *He's gone and left without me.*

The things I found later, in my pockets and in my room, told me that I'd done things only a madwoman or a criminal would've done in such circumstances. I took the filigreed pendant from Chiesa's neck—it turns up in the pocket of my jeans, empty and parted from its chain. At one point I left his rooms with his cigarettes and lighter, put a rolled towel under my bathroom door and with the match I'd struck to light a cigarette I burned my passport in the sink. Already a spill of brown powder—the remnants of Chiesa's caul—had soiled the porcelain. I'd rinsed it all down like dirt, scrubbing the bowl with my fingers.

And then I'd gone back to him, run warm water in a saucepan and washed the line of crusted froth from his mouth. And then I think I stood and shouted at him that I would never forgive him for doing this, for taking himself out of the world so easily and leaving me here alone, because I woke then like a sleepwalker to find myself standing in the middle of Chiesa's bedroom in his misbuttoned shirt, my throat raw and my ears ringing, with running footsteps on the stairs and voices crying *Professoressa, Professoressa!* as if that empty title might bring me back to myself.

My hands had known, at least, to draw the sheet up over his face.

I have the Lancia's keys, but for a day and a night after their unfelt, independent work my hands go limp and motionless, they seem to float on my wrists like seaweed. My hair goes unbrushed, money lies out on the bureau, the lights in my rooms remain dark—my fingers have forgotten how to grasp things, hold things, how to retrieve what's been hidden away. They've burned my passport, those peremptory hands of mine; officers of the carabinieri are on the stairs and in Chiesa's rooms, and my name keeps coming up. They're going to want to see my papers and take a statement, a simple formality until they learn that I have no passport and

I become—as I must—uncooperative. I should leave ahead of their interest in me but my hands are useless as fronds, I can't dig the keys from my purse or even unbolt the door to my rooms. Hotel staff taps at my door but their hearts aren't in it—they leave me alone. I wait for the carabinieri's more determined efforts, but they never come.

The desk clerk must see readily in the dark, like a cat; she shuts my door on the hallway's steady noon and makes her way to me unerringly, a hand touching the back of a chair, a table edge, as if to advise the room of her presence. She bends down, takes me by the arm and pulls me up, puts me in a chair—she's just picking up the room, it seems, looking to straighten the place.

"It smells like arson in here," she says. "Have you burned a hole in the upholstery?"

"No," I say. "I don't know."

She sighs, surveys the room with a kind of detached disgust; she's calculating the man hours needed to clean the place, the time it will take to turn it around for the next guests. Chiesa's shirt has lost all its starch, it's begun to smell like dirty bedsheets on me. I clutch it more tightly around my body.

"The captain of the carabinieri is a sympathetic man, *Professoressa*," the desk clerk says. "He's been known to weep right along with the victims of crimes. I would have told you not to bother embarrassing yourself like this, it isn't necessary . . . what is that down your front? Did you vomit on yourself?"

Even in the dark she can see what happens to my face: it's Chiesa's vomit, not mine.

She leans in over the back of the chair then and holds my face between her hands, strokes my filthy hair while I do not cry. I do not. I simply leave myself instead, I flee my body like a burning city and I go elsewhere for a little while, into a dry countryside strewn with ruins where I can't see Chiesa lying beside me like one already dead—all that Valium and alcohol—his mouth filling with vomit that he can't clear.

The desk clerk waits for me to come back, and I do.

"Besides," she says, "they've completed their investigation. You needn't concern yourself with appearing so broken for them."

She folds her hands on the back of the chair as if she's pushed me away herself.

I stare at her outraged—and horribly relieved. "Who called them off?" I say.

"Well, they're not a pack of dogs, *Professoressa*—no one was baying for your blood. But the captain took a call from the mayor's office, and then I think you must have slipped his mind."

"I slipped his mind."

"Yes. Perhaps he hadn't made a note of it, to talk to you."

"He must not have."

"No."

Her earring catches some minor, errant light, winks faintly.

I get up then. I stand as if from momentary rest, as if I haven't been down for a day and a half like a foundered horse. I shake a cigarette from Chiesa's pack and light it.

In the greater dark that follows the lighter's flare the desk clerk can still find her way across the room. "Well, now you're up," she says from the door. I just nod—she can see.

She'd have left the line open while she went to summon the captain, I think—left the phone off the hook with

Agretta on the other end just to show him his insignificance, to let him listen to the Elimo's ambient bustle and her departing, unhurried footsteps. He'd have been agitated on that call, stung by the Council's panicked recriminations and demands for preemptive action in the wake of Chiesa's death; he's still not entirely well and so would have felt the insult, the danger to himself all the more. Yet when the captain's cool voice comes on the line the mayor matches his to it and becomes plausible; he discourses at length, provides eulogy, rationalization, dissuasion, an exit strategy and, finally, incentive, without ever saying anything of substance, his voice unctuous and unassuming, a little regretful. The captain understands that nothing will be traced back to him, that his career will be advanced. He hangs up the phone and his eyes meet the desk clerk's, and right up until he drops his gaze deliberately to her breasts she thinks that he will surely look away with his unconscionable secret.

Black-bordered hand bills announcing Chiesa's funeral mass appear overnight, pasted on walls over last month's peeling notices. His name is everywhere, calling him as if he were only lost; his absence blows a hole in my heart.

I will always say that the *carrozzóne* that carried Chiesa's coffin to the cemetery was pulled by two mismatched black horses, their coats rusty from the summer's fierce sun. They had black ostrich plumes on their heads, brow bands with long black fringe that curtained their eyes. I'll say that I walked behind the few others in the cortege, keeping my distance; that the ancient japanned hearse rattled stiffly on its old leaf springs, that a smell of liniment fell from the giant eucalyptus trees planted along the cemetery road. Others will say that I wasn't there—they would have marked me in the small crowd, my obvious foreignness, my improper dress. They will insist upon this.

But I say a wind rushed up belatedly as the *carrozzóne* went in the cemetery gate, drawing the eucalyptus trees' long stiff leaves after it; I say the wind roared like water overhead.

I find a use for the revealing blouse and sling-backed heels that were to have provoked unsuspecting librarians on our final crime spree: I wear them into the mayor's office, where Agretta's gaze lights on my skin like a fly. He hides his ill temper in an excess of sympathy recited through clenched teeth. He's still a little jaundiced; his sharkskin suit-coat still laps his body too much. I think I can smell the deals cut in this room, the favors curried—the air smells of whispered speech and cigars, long closed conferences. We're well above the street up here; the bell of the duomo's campanile is just visible from one window, too close and seeming to loiter there, partially hidden. Pigeons shift and flutter among its works.

I tell the mayor that there's something troubling me, an impression I can't shake that needs to be told in confidence to the appropriate authorities, so that I can be rid of it. I tell him that I must unburden myself.

As if I'm a statue ready to fall, Agretta rushes a chair up behind my knees—he wants to catch this confession of mine, prevent me telling it to others. His fingers grip the edge of his steel desktop; he could peel it back like the lid of a tin can, all that anxiety conferring on him a superhuman strength that will last just long enough for him to save himself. He peers intently into my face.

"He's haunting us all," the mayor says. "Tell me your thoughts."

And so I tell him in a long, meandering confidence that I may be imagining things, that at the time I made nothing of certain odd incidents—but now I think perhaps the archivist's death was not an accident.

"Not an—?"

"No. It's crazy, I know," I say, "but I keep thinking that his overdose was deliberate. Because of this trip we took once, and some strange moments that seem to me now like tutelage. I keep thinking—and I know this sounds improbable, that it's likely just the shock of his death affecting my mind—but I keep thinking that he viewed me as his protégé. That he meant for me to take his place."

In the mayor's anteroom someone speaks in monosyllables into the phone; there's the sound of an old adding machine totalling sums. Agretta's smile offers me real violence, strangling or a good beating, maybe—anything to get me to keep my mouth shut. He leans into me, solicitous of my well-being, promising harm.

"But you see what an outlandish notion this is," he says. "This whole ordeal has affected your nerves, *Professoressa*—who wouldn't be in a state? No, it's quite understandable, these wild thoughts coming on the heels of such a shock—"

"I can't bear it," I say. "Everyone thinking he'd made such a monstrous blunder, accidentally overdosing himself. He was incapable of such an error, I'm sure of it."

And then, as if I've just made up my mind
head and say, "No, there's no help for it, Signo
must talk to the captain of the carabinieri."

You can see the sirens go off in his head, tl
eyelids, the twitching, expressionless face. He car
self think over all the panicked screaming, but h
of bureaucratic crises of all kinds. He meets me n
bluntest instruments of persuasion, applies them v

It's all the same to him, his manner suggests, i
I want to do; he leaves me in my chair, goes behi
to take up a few papers, tosses them down. He t
I must do what I think best, of course, but that li
to . . . well, I'll get a sympathetic ear from the c
someone to listen to my story. The captain is a cor
man, he will no doubt feel for me in my distress
what can he do? The inquiry is closed, the family
put this tragedy behind them; can I imagine the
allegations would cause? Suicide! For heaven's sal
poor family have what little consolation an accidei
them. And I've no proof of my claims, anyway—n
these impressions, and really quite honestly the
bit, well, hysterical, if I'll forgive him his bluntnes
think this thing through, Agretta says, consider th
to my reputation, the loss of goodwill I'll incur ii
ceived to be upsetting people needlessly.

I give him a sheep's uncomprehending stare. "
tain will sympathize?" I say.

Oh, I know how it's done, the stolid gaze, the
to arguments offered at any volume or length; I kı
to bend officials. Agretta wants to kill me for it. He
through an elaborate cover of irritable talk and shifted

And so I stand up on those tall stiletto heels an
see my recklessness, the lengths I'll go to; I let him

236

CHAPTER TWENT

And so I go on where I thought I
where I'd come to let things end. I ov
this cursed, continued existence. He
where he stood, with a hand on the
and a winged imp's claws in his back
those kinds of doomed artifacts beloi

And yet I miss him, I miss him s
he must have only set like a moon,
horizon; I still feel the pull of his bod
sure of it, if I could only travel far en
into unseen territory.

My few clothes hanging now in
it look like I've already departed on
behind in haste to speed my travel. I
the dishrag dried stiff over the sink
I am elsewhere; for a time I sleep o
bed with its lithified, twisted sheets,
on the side of the bathroom sink. It
each time I work the faucets, but it's
can't move it. I'm here and I'm not he
a particular departure, a longed–for

238

mine, prevent me telling it to others. His fingers grip the edge of his steel desktop; he could peel it back like the lid of a tin can, all that anxiety conferring on him a superhuman strength that will last just long enough for him to save himself. He peers intently into my face.

"He's haunting us all," the mayor says. "Tell me your thoughts."

And so I tell him in a long, meandering confidence that I may be imagining things, that at the time I made nothing of certain odd incidents—but now I think perhaps the archivist's death was not an accident.

"Not an—?"

"No. It's crazy, I know," I say, "but I keep thinking that his overdose was deliberate. Because of this trip we took once, and some strange moments that seem to me now like tutelage. I keep thinking—and I know this sounds improbable, that it's likely just the shock of his death affecting my mind—but I keep thinking that he viewed me as his protégé. That he meant for me to take his place."

In the mayor's anteroom someone speaks in monosyllables into the phone; there's the sound of an old adding machine totalling sums. Agretta's smile offers me real violence, strangling or a good beating, maybe—anything to get me to keep my mouth shut. He leans into me, solicitous of my well-being, promising harm.

"But you see what an outlandish notion this is," he says. "This whole ordeal has affected your nerves, *Professoressa*—who wouldn't be in a state? No, it's quite understandable, these wild thoughts coming on the heels of such a shock—"

"I can't bear it," I say. "Everyone thinking he'd made such a monstrous blunder, accidentally overdosing himself. He was incapable of such an error, I'm sure of it."

And then, as if I've just made up my mind I shake my head and say, "No, there's no help for it, Signor Agretta—I must talk to the captain of the carabinieri."

You can see the sirens go off in his head, the fluttering eyelids, the twitching, expressionless face. He can't hear himself think over all the panicked screaming, but he's a veteran of bureaucratic crises of all kinds. He meets me now with the bluntest instruments of persuasion, applies them with force.

It's all the same to him, his manner suggests, if that's what I want to do; he leaves me in my chair, goes behind his desk to take up a few papers, tosses them down. He tells me that I must do what I think best, of course, but that little is likely to . . . well, I'll get a sympathetic ear from the captain, yes, someone to listen to my story. The captain is a compassionate man, he will no doubt feel for me in my distress, but really, what can he do? The inquiry is closed, the family wishes to put this tragedy behind them; can I imagine the distress my allegations would cause? Suicide! For heaven's sake! Let the poor family have what little consolation an accident provides them. And I've no proof of my claims, anyway—nothing but these impressions, and really quite honestly they sound a bit, well, hysterical, if I'll forgive him his bluntness. I should think this thing through, Agretta says, consider the damage to my reputation, the loss of goodwill I'll incur if I'm perceived to be upsetting people needlessly.

I give him a sheep's uncomprehending stare. "The captain will sympathize?" I say.

Oh, I know how it's done, the stolid gaze, the deafness to arguments offered at any volume or length; I know how to bend officials. Agretta wants to kill me for it. He stalks me through an elaborate cover of irritable talk and shifted papers.

And so I stand up on those tall stiletto heels and let him see my recklessness, the lengths I'll go to; I let him see that he doesn't stand a chance against me, crippled as he is by his need to preserve himself. It takes him a moment to understand that somehow I've come to have nothing to lose.

"Give me Chiesa's job," I say.

To his credit he drops all his pretense, steps out with a murderous glint in his eyes.

"No," he says.

"Give me his job. I'm a troublemaker, Signor Agretta— I'll go to the carabinieri."

And as if to sound the alarm the hour strikes from the duomo's campanile then, an immoderate, disruptive clanging that the mayor seems to hear as a warning come too late. He looks away, stares after something he knows has escaped him for good.

The bell's reverberations decay to a single, unlovely tone, a residual pressure in the ears.

"He should not have brought you here," Agretta says. "I shouldn't have permitted it."

"No," I say. "But this—what I'm doing now—is why he did it. He knew I had it in me."

A look of thwarted, persistent cunning darkens the mayor's face, a last spasm of willfulness. All I do is sit down, cross my legs, let my skirt ride up.

"Your wife knew he was despondent," I say. "She may even feel a bit responsible for what's happened . . . she was not kind to him in her admirable efforts on your behalf. Have you spoken with her?"

Pigeons are reassembling now on the shoulders of the stilled bell. I watch them instead of the mayor, let his disfiguring rage at what I've done to him go unwitnessed.

"I can't pay you," Agretta says at last.

I give him a brilliant smile. "Sure you can," I say.

CHAPTER TWENTY-EIGHT

And so I go on where I thought I could not, in the place where I'd come to let things end. I owe it to Chiesa, this gift, this cursed, continued existence. He judged me well from where he stood, with a hand on the door of that big Lancia and a winged imp's claws in his back. He knew I'd never let those kinds of doomed artifacts belong to me.

And yet I miss him, I miss him so terribly that it seems he must have only set like a moon, gone below a certain horizon; I still feel the pull of his body. I'd see him again, I'm sure of it, if I could only travel far enough and fast enough, into unseen territory.

My few clothes hanging now in Chiesa's armoire make it look like I've already departed on this journey, items left behind in haste to speed my travel. I leave the kitchen cold, the dishrag dried stiff over the sink's spigot to prove that I am elsewhere; for a time I sleep on the floor beside the bed with its lithified, twisted sheets, I leave Chiesa's razor on the side of the bathroom sink. It threatens my left wrist each time I work the faucets, but it's fixed in place there—I can't move it. I'm here and I'm not here, suspended, awaiting a particular departure, a longed-for reunion. Chiesa knew what would detain me here, all right, that seer, that implacable conniver.

I've abandoned my failed lists, all those names of lost things recorded in false hope of their retrieval; I've swept their pages off the archives desk in a single motion, a wholesale clearing that's sent them to the floor and under shelves, left them impaled on chair legs. I kick through them like drifts of leaves as I take up Chiesa's work, for the pleasure of the sound they make underfoot.

I have the Lancia's faulty ignition module, the black-bound Cadmus. I know what to do with them.

There's a Friday coming that will hum like a tunnel; I'll hear them coming, *Donna* Perchta and her furious horde, I'll feel the wind they push ahead of them. The marks on my arm from Chiesa's needle will have begun to heal by then, and I'll be shaking like a tree, a conduit for every fever dream that's ever been, every possible delirium. In withdrawal de Quincey saw vast processions, dances, battles pass him in darkness, and so will I; on that Friday I'll step out of my body like a parade-goer, into black streets, I'll stand in the path of oncoming grief and let it take me up, carry me headlong. I'll match *Donna* Perchta's killing pace.

And I'll find him. He'll be there among the others, much changed, burdened by all that he's left unconfessed; to console him I'll press my small dark gifts into his hands. If his sins were so great that his arms are full I'll put them to his lips, let him swallow them like food. I'll do this again and again until I lose him to accumulated prayer, to the incremental effects of masses said for his repose.

And then the Advent Embertide will be upon us.

I think Risacca knows what I intend. He invades my dreams now in the body of a prince, tall and richly dressed, staring like a telamon; his appearance incites me to violence, leaves me itching for a fight.

I'll have taken up the needle again by then. So I'll leave it once more, and dream with a vengeance on that Ember Thursday night: of close combat in the air over fields just turned for planting, the smell of opened earth. I'll dream of striking blows, of giving no quarter; and then I'il taunt Risacca on the street as December's black fields turn green.

The weather unravels as winter approaches; frequent rains varnish the town's tiled roofs. The grey sky sinks so low that clouds haunt Valparuta's highest streets, obscuring the view of Trapani to the south and the ocean's blue headlands to the east.

For days we exist by ourselves, answerable to no one.